Lina

For our mother Elsa Dunkelmann,
née Bernhardt.

RUTH ALICE DUNKELMANN

Lina

or

The Short Life of an Exceptional Girl

With advice and support from Brigitte Wege

Bibliographical information of the Deutsche Nationalbibliothek

[German National Library]

Deutsche Nationalbibliothek lists this publication in the Deutsche Nationalbibliografie; detailed bibliographical data may be accessed online at http://dnb.d-nb.de.

© 2021 Ruth Alice Dunkelmann

Graphics: Seita/ Strike Pattern/ Shutterstock.com

Cover design, typesetting, production and publishing:

BoD – Books on Demand, Norderstedt

ISBN 978-3-7543-9258-4

Contents

Foreword

Aunt Gertrud's 85th birthday is being celebrated in Schwäbisch Hall in October 2010. Numerous well-wishers arrive and the stream of visitors seems to have no end.

After lunch, everyone waits for coffee. The excitement has died down a little and Aunt Gertrud leans back and relaxes. "Yes, yes, we used to be ten siblings, now there are only the three of us," she says to her two sisters Hanna and Elsa. Everyone present nods thoughtfully, then all the names and dates of birth are listed. This is not at all easy, especially since the siblings did not grow up together – some of them only met when they were adults.

Once again I take this opportunity to ask about Lina. But today, too, I only get a short, vague reply: "The Nazis killed all the disabled people back then." And it's not the first time I have heard this. I try to ask more questions, but quickly give up, as I realize that none of the sisters knows anything more about Lina's fate.

"You would have had to ask Liesl," my mother says. Aunt Liesl was the oldest of the siblings, and died years ago.

I am very much annoyed that I didn't ask earlier. "It's really sad that no one remembers Lina anymore," I say to my mother. "After all, she was your sister and my aunt."

The thought of Lina haunts me persistently from then on. Finally, I set off in earnest in search of her.

On the internet I come across the Deaconry in Stetten, where Lina is mentioned at a memorial service. Her medical records do indeed still exist there. There are also a few lines about Lina and her siblings in Lichtenstern. Finally, old lists stored in the state archives in Ludwigsburg also prove helpful.

At this point, I would like to take the opportunity to thank Mr. Reiff of the archives office in Stetten, Mrs. Richter from the Lichtenstern Protestant Foundation and the friendly staff at the Ludwigsburg State Archives. They helped me a lot, in the end almost all my questions were answered. Unfortunately, in all this research I did not find even a single photo that could be unmistakably identified as a picture of Lina. But at least now, more than 70 years after her death, she has finally acquired a face and a voice.

Ruth Alice Dunkelmann, February 2019

History

Based on belief in the doctrine of racial hygiene, people with disabilities and mental illnesses were exposed to discrimination and persecution at an early stage under National Socialism. From January 1934, they were subjected to forced sterilization on the basis of the Law for the Prevention of Hereditary Diseases. Approximately 400,000 people suffered this fate by the end of the war, and about 5,000 died as a result of the operations.

By the summer of 1939 at the latest, the decision had been taken in Hitler's entourage to destroy mentally handicapped and mentally ill people as "lives unworthy of life".

The murders, which the perpetrators called "euthanasia", were systematically planned. Within the framework of various murder campaigns (e.g. "Action T4", "Reich Committee Children", "Action 14f13" or "Second Murder Phase"), approximately 300,000 people lost their lives under the National Socialist tyranny between autumn 1939 and the end of the war in 1945.

In "Action T4", approximately 70,000 people were murdered in the gas chambers of six killing centers between January 1940 and August 1941. The last of these to be built was the Hadamar killing center. Approximately 10,000 patients were killed in its gas chamber between January and August 1941. After a break of one year, the former Hadamar state sanatorium resumed its function as a killing center. As such, it was integrated into the "Second Murder Phase", in which murders were carried out primarily with overdosed medication and targeted malnutrition. From August 1942 until the end of the war, another 4,500 people died in Hadamar.

(http://www.gedenkstaette-hadamar.de, accessed 28.07.2012)

In the parental home

It is summer of the year 1926. Two-year-old Lina lies on her bed and moans quietly. Everything hurts her, especially the right side of her body hurts unbearably. Hunger and thirst also torment her, but that is nothing new for Lina.

"Mommy," she cries feebly and babbles unintelligibly to herself. She hasn't learned to speak yet, she only knows a few simple words that she can hardly remember now. She stares intently at the door.

Liesl, who is seven years old, finally comes in. Lina beams at her sister and calls out, "Yoo-hoo."

"Yes, I know you're hungry," Liesl says. "Here, drink your tea, mother made it specially for you."

Lina reaches for the cup and for Liesl's hand. "Stay wi - ," she stammers and tries to hold the girl with her gaze.

"I can't stay, I have to go out again," Liesl explains. "The lady next door will give me a some bread and jam if I hang out her washing, I'll bring some for you." And already she is out the door.

For long days, Lina lies on the bed in the kitchen. Most of the time she is asleep or dozing. When she is awake, she stares at the door and waits for Liesl or her brother Fritz. Only in the evening does her mother come home with her little sister.

At night Liesl snuggles into bed with her. This makes Lina happy because she doesn't like to be alone. Liesl tells her what she has done and seen all day. One day she whispers a secret in her ear: "Soon we'll have another little brother, because the other one has gone back to the dear Savior." Lina nods, silently moved; she finds this incredibly exciting.

Sometimes her mother pushes the basket with little Gertrud in it next to the girls' bed. Lina can't get enough of the tiny hands and the sweet little face. She tries again and again to stroke the baby, but her hand hurts too much and won't move properly.

Lina has a fever, a high temperature. Her mother takes her to the Deaconry Hospital in Schwäbisch Hall.

Anxiously, Lina opens her eyes. It is very bright all around her. A large room with white walls, and the people are also dressed in white.

A man leans over her and stares into her face. Lina cries out in fright. Fortunately, her mother is there to hold her in her arm.

"It's all right, Lina," she says softly, "don't get upset, the doctor will make you feel better soon."

The doctor looks rather stern. "Polio, probably. That's not good, it's bound to leave its mark; I suppose she's already had measles," he murmurs. The mother nods.

Lina is very hot and can't keep her eyes open any longer. In her fever she fantasizes, dreams of little children and of her little brother in heaven playing with the angels.

At home she is startled out of sleep by loud shouts. It is her father shouting: "What a pigsty, this is no way to live! And there's nothing decent to eat either! No wonder the children are sick!"

"What am I supposed to cook with if you don't bring

any money home? You have to take it all to the pub and pour it down your throat!" her mother yells back just as loudly.

Lina stretches out her arms to her father, but he doesn't see her. Today he probably won't sit at the table with her and feed her. Otherwise he does that often and Lina loves it, even if her mother thinks she should feed herself – but it's just too hard for her with her bad hand.

Fritz sits at the kitchen table and cries quietly. He is six years old and has just started school; he doesn't like it much. Today the teacher gave him a beating because he still didn't have a notebook. His mother didn't want to buy him one – he shouldn't need one in the first grade, she said.

"But I *do* need a notebook now," Fritz whines as the door loudly slams shut. His father bangs his way down the stairs and slams the door at the bottom as well.

"Yes, run away – you just do that, and leave me with all the misery!" the mother shouts after him through the window. "And you," she turns to Fritz, "you tell your teacher that we don't have any money for this nonsense. What do you have a slate for! And now I don't want to hear another word about it, do you understand?"

Fritz says nothing in reply. But he will get a notebook. The neighbors give him things now and then if he asks them very nicely. Or he will ask Liesl, maybe she will give him a few pages from her notebook. He knows that he has to help himself, because there is no talking to his mother today. He can see that from her red face and the strange gleam in her eyes.

Mother and father

Marie Luise and Friedrich Bernhardt were married on 17 August 1918. It was a wartime wedding, Friedrich was briefly home on leave. A few months later the war ended and their life together could begin.

Marie Luise was born as the daughter of a maid in Enslingen near Schwäbisch Hall. Her mother was unmarried, which was quite a disgrace at the time. Luise was certainly made to feel it throughout her childhood. Friedrich came from a large family in Flossholz, a tiny village in the forest not far from Schwäbisch Hall.

Perhaps they met at a village festival or worked for the same farmer? In the family register there are no more than a few dates and names that we can only barely bring to life with the help of the imagination.

After the wedding they moved to Steinbach (now a district of Schwäbisch Hall). Neither of them received anything from home other than a few good words of advice. What they need to live, they had to earn for themselves.

Friedrich works in factories, and sometimes in the quarry. The work is very hard and the pay is always insufficient. They only buy the most necessary household goods for a small modest apartment.

After work, Friedrich often goes to the inn. A beer doesn't cost the earth and there are pubs on every corner. The other boys and girls from the village also meet there.

They all know each other and can spend a few convivial hours together.

Luise comes along occasionally, but most of the time she has to work long hours for the local farmers, especially in the summer. There is cider to drink and always too little to eat. "A good cider is better than nothing, leave water to the cows," the other farmhands and maids laugh.

Even if the cider is heavily diluted, Luise soon notices the effect of the alcohol, especially as she hardly has anything in her stomach. Actually, she doesn't find it all that unpleasant. The dullness of everyday life and the never-ending work are easier to put up with. Everything becomes a bit easier and more bearable. The many major and minor worries fade into the background and it is easier to laugh.

1919 to 1926

Soon she knows that she is expecting a child. The fact that it is born "in wedlock" is very important for Luise, because she has not yet forgotten the teasing she was subjected to. Her children will not have to endure this "disgrace", at least she has made sure of that. Money is tight, but the children will always have a father.

If only Friedrich would not be so careless with money. Time and again he loses his job, he is simply not consistent enough. He is always finding fault with his employers or the foremen. Luise herself knows that the farmers are often "pigs", but what can you do? There are so many people looking for work, especially now after the war. So you just have to suck it up and carry on. Luise is used to that. But Friedrich is different, he just won't take it lying down.

The first child is a girl. She was to be called Luise, like the mother, but everyone calls her "Liesl". The parents are very happy and the father says: "That's good, the next one will be a boy. Liesl can look after him right away."

And he is proved right. Liesl is barely one year old when the father is able to pass on his name to his first son. For the sake of simplicity, he is called "Fritz".

The little family could actually be content and happy now, because two healthy children are a blessing. But they also make a lot of work. Luise cannot go on working at the farmer's, because she can hardly take both children with her.

Money is tight, Friedrich is out of work again. If he shows up at home at all, he usually complains that the children are not being properly looked after. The house is never clean enough for him either. But Luise finds everything even more of a struggle. She strokes her swollen belly sadly.

Liesl has just turned four and Fritz is not yet three when another boy is born: Karl. Not only did Luise have a difficult birth with him, the midwife said straight away: "Oh dear, he won't be up to much." Little Karl is very weak and doesn't want to eat or grow properly.

Even at two years old, he has not developed very well. But the mother can look after him even less now, because Karoline, called "Lina", has come along in the meantime. It is almost impossible for Luise to look after everyone. Because she has to stay at home, she gets home work, stuffing sacks. A boring job for which she at least gets a few pennies. But that is just a drop in the ocean.

Then the two little children get sick with measles. A catastrophe. The mother quickly sends Liesl and Fritz to stay with the neighbors.

The little ones are not at all well, especially Karl is getting weaker and weaker. They even have to call the doctor, the midwife had insisted. There was nothing more she could do, she said.

But it is too late. Karl doesn't make it, he dies at the age of two and a half. "He went back to the dear Savior," the mother explains to the siblings. "Maybe that wasn't such a bad idea."

1927

Finally Lina is allowed to get up again and she is actually feeling a little better. The paralysis in her right hand and right leg has remained, but she is still cheerful. She no longer even knows what she is missing.

She sits with Liesl and little Gertrud on the stairs in front of the house. Happily, she waggles her head and sings: "Comes a birdie a-flying …" "Don't act so stupid," Liesl scolds her, "you're not a moron!" Lina hugs little Gertrud and continues to sing softly into her ear. The baby is delighted and pats her face exuberantly.

"Hush," Liesl says, "can't you hear our new little brother screaming?" The children listen intently, and Fritz has now also sat down on the steps. It is 12 December and not very cozy outside, but the midwife has sent everyone out. "Has the Christ Child brought the little brother?" asks Lina suddenly. The children look at each other inquiringly. "But that would be a silly present," Fritz finally says.

In fact, as it turns out, their little brother Emil is born on this day. This does not make things easier for the family – on the contrary. In spring, the mother goes back to work with the farmers, taking little Emil with her. The other children are locked up in the kitchen at home. There is no other way.

The mother twists the oven door shut with wire so they can't get at it. She also tells the children not to go near the skylight and never to open it. To scare them, she tells them about a man with a long hook who pulls children out of the skylight. Fearfully, the siblings keep looking up at the skylight to see if perhaps they will see "the Hook Goblin".

Often Liesl and Fritz just don't go to school, which their mother doesn't think is so bad. It's better for them to look after their little brothers and sisters at home – especially Lina, who is no longer quite "right" after her illness, as Luise sometimes says. That was just what they needed.

The children are locked in the kitchen all day and hungry as usual. When they discover the sugar tin, they greedily stick their fingers into it and almost lick it empty. Their mother gives them a massive telling off when she discovers the theft, and forbids them to go near it ever again.

At first they stick to it. But when they get too hungry, Fritz fishes for the can and immediately makes a face. "Baah! Yuck!" he cries, startled, and pushes the can back again. His mother has filled it with salt, and hidden the sugar somewhere else. This quite takes away their appetite for sugar.

Every now and then, the children are locked up for quite a long time. They do not always keep quiet, which does not go unnoticed by the neighbors. Many families are in a similar situation and actually have enough to do with their own domestic misery. But Luise's family is not spared. People "talk" about the Bernhardts – too much is "out of order" there. Fritz is always begging for bread from the neighbors: "For my little sister," he says, "she has been so sick."

Truancy is no longer tolerated. Liesl and Fritz's teachers contact the school authorities, and do not omit to mention the children's neglected appearance. They have already been the subject of talk about missing homework and inadequate school performance for a long time.

Again, the children are sitting tired and hungry in the kitchen. Their mother's way home takes her past many hostelries. Actually she only goes in to look for Friedrich. But then she often has a drink herself, and sometimes one too many.

The neighbors see her finally come home and start to gossip. Inside, hungry children are waiting, dirty clothes, a mountain of unwashed dishes and there is not enough food by any stretch of the imagination. Everything is always dirty, the children's clothes are so torn that Luise doesn't know where to start mending them. The household is getting to be too much for her.

To make matters worse, Friedrich has also been caught "stealing". Actually, he only took what was rightfully his, he thinks. Because the farmer didn't pay him properly for his drudgery, Friedrich took a sack of potatoes with him – they were all happy about it at home. But now the nasty farmer has turned him in.

The local beadle has already been here a few times, but Friedrich always disappeared quickly and wouldn't even talk to him. Today the beadle comes again and looked around the habitation, shaking his head. "If things don't look better here soon, I'll have to call the Youth Welfare Office," he says. "And what use are the Youth Welfare

Office people? They're not going to shell out a thing for us," Luise complains.

When he has gone, she tries to tidy up a bit while the children are asleep. She hangs a few clothes on the line that is stretched across the kitchen. She will wash the dirty dishes tomorrow, because she suddenly doesn't feel well at all. She crosses the street again briefly to get herself a tot at the inn.

Spring 1929

Luise holds her aching back and straightens up. "Phew," she moans, "this beet hoeing is really one of the worst jobs. Always bending over to get at the weeds, you feel like your back is going to give way."

"You can say that again. And in your condition, too," nods Martha, who works next to her and occasionally helps to hoe Luise's rows. "How many kids does that make?" she asks.

"Six," says Luise, considering. "Oh, no, actually seven," she corrects herself immediately, "there was Karl who died."

"Whew, you could slow down a bit," Martha says bluntly. "Otherwise you'll end up like me and they'll take your kids away.' Martha continues furiously to hack at the weeds, occasionally bending down to pull out a few clumps by hand.

"Yes, when there isn't a father in the picture, it can happen," says Luise reflectively. "They should have given you a few marks for decent clothes and a sack of potatoes, then your children would still be at home where they belong. – But things will soon be looking up for us," she continues cheerfully, "Friedrich has the prospect of a good job at the factory."

Martha just nods and looks at her doubtfully.

In the evening Luise waits a long time for Friedrich. He should have asked at the factory again today. It would be so good for him to finally find work. Especially now that the social services and the youth welfare office are breathing down their necks.

Just yesterday Liesl said, "There was a nice lady here who brought us sweet rolls and milk and asked how school was going." "What's that you say?" Luise snapped at her. "How many times have I told you not to open the door?" "But she said if we didn't open it, she'd call the police," Liesl defended herself. "Besides, Emil was screaming so much that I got scared. But then she was quite nice to us."

Luise had been very much alarmed. She fears the worst.

Friedrich still doesn't come home. She can't go and look for him herself, her feet and back are not up to it. Carefully, she rouses her son. Fritz is not happy about it. He grumbles and mutters under his breath, but finally he sets off.

He already knows all the inns in the vicinity. Luckily he finds his father in the first one. "Hey, Fritzle, what are you doing in the alley at this time of night?" Friedrich asks happily when he sees the boy. "Mother says it's time for you to come home," Fritz mumbles, exhausted. His father finishes his beer and they leave immediately.

On the way home, Friedrich slips him a few sweets and tells him: "That factory job won't work out, they only hire better people with skills. The bosses there are all criminals and cutthroats. Someone like me doesn't stand a chance," he complains. "At least I liberated a set of spanners, they don't need so many if they don't employ people. But don't say a word to your mother!"

Bravely, Lina tries to run along with her siblings and the neighbors' children, but she soon falls far behind.

Her leg just won't do what she wants it to. "Wait for me!" she shouts after the others, but they don't want to be always waiting for Lina. Besides, she can't really join in their games.

Sadly, Lina limps home again. There she sees two young cats playing with each other in the street. They try to catch each other's tails and run clumsily around in circles. Lina has to laugh again, waving her arms in the air with joy.

She is never sad for long and gets distracted by every little thing. But she also finds it difficult to stay on the ball for long and to remember things. No sooner has her mother told her to do something than Lina has already forgotten it.

As Lina approaches the house, she hears loud shouting. She can't understand what it's about, but her parents seem very upset. Startled, she stops on the stair and wags her head nervously (she always does this when she is upset or at a loss).

Suddenly the front door bursts open and a man in uniform and cap comes out. He stomps quickly and vigorously down the stairs. He almost knocks Lina over, who is pressing herself anxiously against the wall of the house. Then he notices her and looks her up and down: "Are you another one of the criminals in there?" he yells at the girl. Lina continues to wobble her head and stares at the man with wide eyes. She is too frightened to answer. "Can't even speak," he continues, "are you some kind of retard?" He makes a dismissive gesture with his hand and hurries on.

In the kitchen, her mother is sitting at the table and crying. Lina huddles up against her and strokes her hair. "Oh Lina, these are not good times for poor people like us," the mother moans.

The Bernhardt family are not exceptional, many others are in the same boat. The consequences of the war can still be felt in Schwäbisch Hall and hardship is present everywhere. War-damaged, malnourished children and adults are everywhere to be seen in town. Unemployment, hunger, social misery lead to a criminalization of everyday life, people fight for bare survival. Thefts of food and even raids on shops are not unusual. People are desperate and do not know what to do to help themselves.

1 October 1929

Excited, the siblings push each other away from the window to see better. "That's a Ford," Fritz yells, "an ambulance!"

Liesl turns quite pale and says quietly: "That's it, now they're coming for us!"

Lina clings to her right arm. With her left hand Liesl tries to hold onto Gertrud, who starts to cry terribly. The little girl is quite incapable of consolation, she seems to sense the fear of the others.

There has been a lot of talk about "taking away" lately. Lina heard their parents talking about it and told Liesl. She said that something like that was also written in the letters she secretly read.

Footsteps are already approaching the house. Liesl opens the door and stops with her arms hanging down and a submissive expression on her face. The man who met Lina on the stairs comes in, and behind him the woman who has already brought them some food once before.

"Come, children," she says kindly, "we're going for a drive in a nice car, and you'll get cake too." Gertrud promptly stops crying.

The children are completely stunned, but also mute with fear. None of them had ever sat in a car before. Fritz has only ever talked about cars, he knows a lot about them and is very interested in them. Now he presses his forehead against the window and hiccups with sheer excitement.

During the drive, the woman gives them cake and even lemonade. She talks to the children all the time, tells them about a beautiful big garden where they can play and about the many other children who are already waiting for them.

At some point Liesl dares to ask quietly: "Where are we actually going?"

"Oh, to Lichtenstern, to the children's home, of course," comes the reply.

Liesl has already heard about it – the children of Martha, mother's friend, are also there. But they no longer have a father, he was killed in the war. Martha has often said that her daughter Klara is always homesick.

"Yes, but what about father and mother?" asks Liesl.

"They have another little child now, so they can't look after you any more. But they will visit you soon," the woman explains.

"Friedele," says Lina softly and Liesl nods.

Their new baby sister was born just a few days ago. That's why their mother took her to the hospital today for a check-up, and took Emil with her. Their mother has been very tired lately and unable to get out of bed.

They have been driving for quite a while, often through a forest, past meadows and fields. Rarely do they encounter another car. Then they go down some steep bends and through the forest again. Fritz is starting to feel sick, he has already turned quite pale. "We'll be there soon," says the driver.

In the distance they see a few houses and a wall, situated on a hill and surrounded by gardens and fields. "That's Lichtenstern, you'll be fine there," says the lady.

The car drives through the archway and stops in front of a large half-timbered house. An elderly woman with an apron and a headscarf is already waiting for them. "Is that them?" is all she says.

The children don't quite know what's happening to them. Before they know it they are in a large bathroom and the woman with the apron and a younger blonde woman are busy with them. They take off their clothes and brush their hair.

Liesl suddenly notices that Fritz is no longer there. "Where is my brother?" she asks the blonde woman, who seems friendlier than the other.

"With the boys, of course," the older one snaps at her, "what do you expect? We have discipline and order here – now just take off your lice-ridden clothes and into the tub with you!"

Liesl climbs into the bathtub without a murmur, but Lina struggles and screams. She flutters her arms and waggles her head from side to side.

"What's her problem?" asks the older woman. "Is she not right in the head?"

"She's just scared and agitated," Liesl says and jumps out of the tub again. She takes Lina in her arms and tries to calm her down. "Besides, she has been very sick," she adds angrily.

The blonde woman finally puts all three girls in a bath tub and combs out their hair. It hurts and the children moan. "All full of lice," she says, giving herself a shake.

Their brother Fritz is no better off. He is taken to another house by a severe gentleman in a suit. There his head is simply shaved, and he too is put into a bath tub. He feels very strange without his sisters, but he bites his lip bravely and does not cry.

When at dinner he sees them again, he hardly recognizes them. The girls have tightly braided plaits and strange, clean clothes. He is about to run over to them, but the teacher has already grabbed him by the collar: "No way. You sit at the table with me and the boys! Or are you just a girl and a crybaby, eh?" The other boys laugh spitefully.

Many small children, and bigger ones as well, are sitting in the dining room. They all stare curiously at the "newbies". Despite their nervousness, they are very hungry, and the siblings make the most of the food set before them.

When the girls see the dormitory with its many beds, they can't help but be amazed. "There are thirty beds!" says Liesl, who has quickly counted them. The beds are close together, there are no other furnishings, there just wouldn't be any room.

As usual, the three sisters climb into bed together. But strict Auntie Sofie, whom they have already met at dinner, forbids them. "Whatever are you up to? With us, everyone sleeps in their own bed, OK?" The girls of course do what she says. But as soon as Auntie Sofie turns off the light, Lina quickly slips into bed with her little sister. Gertrud is crying again. Tired and confused, she clings to Lina. "Shh, Gertrudle," whispers Lina softly.

The living situation in Fritz's "boys' house" is similar. Here too there is a large dormitory that is well occupied. But he is all alone, and the other boys are mean to him because they are always mean to the "newbies". That's just the way it is.

Sadly, he thinks of home and wonders what his parents are doing now. Maybe mother has had to stay in the hospital with the two little ones? Or perhaps she is sitting at home and crying… In that case their father must have gone to the pub, because he can't stand it. What will they do now without the older children? And what about his friends, Karl and Schorsch? They will wait for him tomorrow in vain. He didn't even get to say goodbye to them. Hopefully Liesl is right and the parents will pick them up again soon. He doesn't want to stay here. Tired and despairing, Fritz cries himself silently to sleep.

Lichtenstern, October 1929 to June 1931

Next morning the world already looks a bit friendlier. It is a beautiful clear autumn day and the woods around Lichtenstern are resplendent with all colors. The siblings go for a walk and view the grounds.

"Such a beautiful, big church – just for children," Liesl marvels. Later she will find out more about the history of Lichtenstern and learn that it is located in a former monastery.

The monastery of Lichtenstern was founded in 1242 by Countess Luitgard of Weinsberg. In addition to the monastery church (1280) which still exists today, the monastery complex, which was built by the end of the 13th century, included the cloister with its beautiful tracery and ribbed vaulting, the convent building, residential accommodation for about 25 nuns and outbuildings. The monastery experienced its heyday in the 15th century.

After 300 years of existence, the monastery was dissolved by Duke Christoph in 1554 in the course of the Reformation. He established a monastery superintendency, which administered the properties and benefices of the former monastery. During this time, the Oberamtei (as an extension of the church) and the Bandhaus (1586) were built, which today, together with the church, the Forsthaus and Binderhaus, form the medieval ensemble of Lichtenstern.

In 1836, citizens from Löwenstein (the Schmidgall

brothers), together with the physician Justinus Kerner and Pastor Hegler, founded an association and a foundation to open a Children's Rescue Home in the former Cistercian monastery of Lichtenstern. The impetus for this was given by Carl August Zeller, who based the educational project on the spirit of Pestalozzi. Giving children and young people future prospects was the goal of the institution until after the Second World War. Until the 1960s, Lichtenstern was a children's home before it became a facility for the disabled in 1963.

(http://www.lichtenstern.de,
accessed: 10.07.2012)

"Look, there are Klara and Werner!" Liesl exclaims. She waves excitedly to the two. They have known them for a long time, because they are the children of mother's friend Martha. They are delighted to see each other again, especially when Klara fetches their cousin August. Fritz almost gushes with excitement: "It's so great that you are here too, August!" At last he has a friend again.

Today the children set out together for a journey of discovery. First they walk through the beautiful monastery garden, which is located right next to the boys' house, then on over the hill. They cheerfully explore their new home.

To begin with, Lina and Gertrud cling to Liesl all the time. Time and again, Lina asks about their mother and father, about little brother Emil and the new tiny sister. Liesl gradually loses patience with her. They have only been in Lichtenstern for a few days, but she has already explained things to Lina ever so many times.

"But I told you before," she says, irritated, "we're just going to have to stay here for a while. Our parents will come and pick us up. After all, we do still have parents, not like most of the children here who don't have any, or only have a mother or a father. You have to be good now, and not always be fidgeting or wagging your head, because they don't like that here," she explains earnestly.

Lina nods and tries to be good. But everything is so new and disturbing that it's hard for her to stay calm.

Liesl has her hands full with her two little sisters – they stick to her like burrs. When she comes home from school, Gertrud and Lina are already eagerly waiting for her. Most of the time they sit on the low wall in front of the girls' house and let their legs dangle.

Liesl also has to help them both at mealtimes, because the "aunties" already have their hands full with the other little children. At first, the caregivers didn't take it in that Lina can't feed herself – after all, she is nearly six years old. But they soon realize that something is not quite right. Liesl is now allowed to help her after all.

The children at last have enough to eat and are no longer hungry all the time. They like pretty much everything, they really aren't choosy – except when it happens to be "Hutzel porridge" (boiled dried fruit with semolina). Liesl feels sick just looking at this strange slimy concoction. The semolina porridge is okay, and she eats it up quickly. She simply leaves the rest on her plate and hopes that no one will notice. Unfortunately, she hasn't allowed for strict Auntie Sofie.

"That's not how we do things here," the latter says severely. "You always eat up everything that is on your plate, or no one is allowed out to play. So make sure you finish every mouthful, Liesl."

The other girls give her dirty looks, and Jule, sitting nearby, hisses, "Eat up, we want to play tag."

Liesl bravely puts a spoon in her mouth and swallows without chewing, "Uahhh …" She almost spits out the tough, squishy mass again, she is so disgusted and feels like crying. But then it occurs to her that after all she has two little sisters sitting next to her! And in a flash, as soon as Aunt Sofie isn't looking, she puts a big spoonful of Hutzel mush into each of their mouths. The two of them wrinkle their noses indignantly, but dutifully swallow it all.

"Well done, Liesl." Aunt Sofie is happy, when the plate is finally empty. Cheerfully, they all skip and jump out into the garden.

"You're a sly one," says Jule. She grins at Liesl and links arms with her.

The days at Lichtenstern pass in an orderly and well structured way. This is something the Bernhardt children are not used to. At home, there were no structures, and hardly any order or rules. It is not easy for them to fit into the thoroughly organized daily routine. Fritz, in particular, is having a hard time with it; he is always late or messes up the day's agenda. In addition, now that he finally has a few friends, he thinks the time allowed for playing and romping is always much too short.

In the first few days the siblings have been thoroughly examined. All of them had lice and also bug bites. In addition, they were quite neglected, dirty and malnourished, but that after all was pretty much par for the course. Otherwise Liesl, Gertrud and Fritz are healthy. Liesl admittedly is a bit small and weak for her age, but she has no serious health problems. With Lina it is quite different – she is most definitely not "normal".

Report from Lichtenstern (1929) about Lina:

Mentally very weak, right-sided paralysis originating from the brain
Prognosis: not hopeful
Needy for love, cuddly, friendly, extremely nervous, hasty and restless, great need for recognition. Psyche very low. Still cannot speak clearly, has difficulty expressing herself with her own peculiar word formations. Healthy, blooming appearance.

As for the reasons why the children have been brought here, we find the following stated:

Sad family circumstances, father often drunk, rarely at home, with a recidivist criminal record for theft. Mother also very prone to drinking, exercises a shameful influence on the children.

The Inspector (director) of the Lichtenstein facility thoughtfully shakes his head: "Lina must be examined again very thoroughly when she has settled in a bit. There seems to be quite a bit wrong with her. I also need to get more detailed information about her previous illnesses," he tells the nurse in an undertone. Under his breath he adds, "I hardly think we can keep her here with us in Lichtenstern permanently. Surely she would be better off in a home for special needs in the long run, but we won't decide that today."

Winter is slowly coming on. The children like slipping into their beds in the evening and are happy about the extra wool blankets. It's always too cold in the old building, especially in the dormitory. Just getting up is a torment, and washing in the morning is even more so. Hot water is a luxury that is rarely available. All the girls have to wash at a long stone trough on which a multitude of wash bowls are lined up. The "aunties" stand alongside and watch them with an eagle eye. Lina needs help most of the time – the paralysis in her right hand has not improved and there are many things she simply cannot manage to do.

When the first snow falls, the siblings are once again amazed. Here in the midst of nature and near the forest, everything looks like a fairytale world. In the mornings and evenings, the freshly fallen snow seems to literally glisten on the trees. As soon as the lessons are over, the children can't be stopped, no matter how cold it is. They rush out into the white world, build snow castles, igloos and snowmen.

Lina loves to throw herself backwards and make angels in the snow. She romps around outside with abandon. Because of her cheerful nature, she has already made a few friends. She is especially fond of Auntie Emma, the young blonde care worker. Lina is always running after her like a puppy and adores her. Auntie Emma laughs and says, "Oh, there's my poor little black cat again," and strokes Lina's dark hair. This makes Lina happy – she beams like the sun.

An elderly woman who helps out in the kitchen from time to time is another of Lina's favorites. Time and again she sneaks into the kitchen and sings "Comes a birdie a-flying" to her. As she sings she jumps, dances and waves her arms. The old woman laughs until tears come to her eyes. This makes Lina even happier, because she loves having an "audience".

In December, a large fir tree is brought into the church. Two men and two boys labor to shift it, while the girls stand around and watch.

"That's a really big Christmas tree," Klara marvels. "Last Christmas was just wonderful," she tells the siblings, "candles everywhere, and everything so beautifully festive. This evening we can start making stars and we won't have to stuff stockings or knit again for a while."

When evening comes, Lina is very sad because she can't do any handicrafts – for that you need to have dexterous fingers. The other girls sit comfortably at the table and busily make stars out of straw. Lina only distracts everyone, she tries to help out everywhere and be involved. But she just gets everything mixed up, or throws the straw off the table.

"Lina, that's enough! If you don't stop, you'll go to the dormitory all by yourself. Sit down quietly and watch," Auntie Sofie scolds. But that is impossible for Lina. She can't sit still at all, she's always on the move, she wants this and then that and has already forgotten it again.

"We can't go on like this for much longer with that child," Sofie says quietly to Emma. "Lina will probably have to go to Mariaberg or Stetten, she's just too much trouble here. They have more staff there and are better equipped for dealing with that kind of child."

"Oh no, the poor little thing, she's so funny," Emma says and takes Lina on her lap. She laughs again and says: "Little black kitten."

At Christmas, the church is beautifully decorated, with straw stars hanging everywhere. Lights glitter on the fir tree and the organ plays even more beautifully than usual.

"Silent Night, Holy Night" the children sing and, for a wonder, Lina sings along properly without forgetting the words. Songs and music quickly enter her soul and lodge in her memory. She stands in the church full of emotion, and her eyes shine. She wishes the organ would never stop playing.

Christmas in Lichtenstern is wonderful. There is a special feast, and some sweets and even a few small presents are distributed. When the girls are sent to the dormitory in the evening, they are very happy, but also very tired. Lina is almost asleep when she hears Auntie

Emma say to Liesl: "Tomorrow your parents are coming to visit you."

On Christmas Day, the parents really arrive, and they have even brought baby Frieda with them. Lina is almost giddy with excitement and immediately asks about her "little brother".

"Well, would you believe it, they took Emil away too," the mother explains quietly. "He's living with a couple who don't have any children of their own, I'm sure he's fine there. We're going tomorrow to see how he's doing."

"My goodness, you've grown!" Lina's father laughs and hoists her over his head with both arms. "I can hardly lift you any more." The girl squeaks with delight. But Gertrud has already become quite a "stranger". She keeps trying to hide behind Liesl.

The parents have brought a few treats and Christmas cookies, but the children are not as greedy for them as they used to be. Here they have enough to eat, and they are not short of sweet things. The mother admires the girls' clean aprons and neatly braided plaits. Fritz also looks so clean that she can't quite get used to it.

"When can we come home again?" Fritz asks his father.

"Ah, lad, if it were only that simple. You wouldn't believe it, the headaches we've had with the department. When they once get you by the throat, they aren't ever going to leave off. Ordinary folks and simple citizens like us are just powerless." Fritz doesn't understand any of this, but his father looks so sad that he doesn't dare ask any more questions.

Today is visiting day and many people are wandering

around the place, mostly parents or relatives of the children who are being looked after. Luise and Friedrich also have a guided tour of the facility and take a close look at everything.

"Do you like it here, Lina?" asks her mother. Lina skips cheerfully along beside her and holds her hand tight.

"Yes, like it, and Auntie Emma, she nice," Lina beams.

"You must speak properly and clearly, Lina, otherwise you won't be able to go to school next year." Her mother looks at her doubtfully.

"Oh well, Lina always likes everything," Liesl interrupts. "It's not that great here. Aunt Sofie isn't nice at all, and the food isn't always good either! Yes, it was great at Christmas, but otherwise … We have to darn socks all the time and …" Liesl lists everything she doesn't like, including having to look after the two little ones all the time. Finally she has a chance to get it all off her chest …

"But you must stick together," their mother explains to her, "you do know after all how sick Lina has been."

Worry lines crisscross Luise's forehead. Just what will become of Lina? She thinks with horror of the meeting she and Friedrich were invited to this morning with the Inspector in his office. "Hereditary imbecility and mental weakness," the Inspector said. Luise explained to him carefully that Lina had contracted polio and measles: "That's what caused the paralysis in the right half of her body, and she probably also suffered slight brain damage," Luise admits. "But all my other children are perfectly healthy, so how can it be hereditary or congenital?"

The Inspector didn't ask any more questions. He just

said that it was not yet clear what was best for Lina. Above all, he said, she couldn't be "accommodated" in school and so was not "viable" for the children's home in the long run.

Of course Friedrich got angry at this point and shouted: "Then we'll take her home right away! We think she's very viable." On his way out, he slammed the door unnecessarily loudly.

All too soon the visiting day draws to a close. The parents have to leave early because it's a long way to the train station in Affaltrach. Together with Martha, who has also visited her children, they slowly prepare to depart in the afternoon. Luise holds little Gertrud in her arms – at last the girl has thawed out a little – and then they have to leave again. She quickly hugs Friedel – at least she can take this little girl home with her.

"Be good and take care of each other," the parents admonish them as they leave. "We'll be back soon," the father calls, as the parents are already walking down the hill. The children, including Martha's two, stand at the top, and wave until the parents have disappeared around the bend.

Everyday life in Lichtentern with its many small duties quickly resumes. The Bernhardt children have settled in well, and the two older ones go to school. The teachers have a hard time with them – not just with them, but with the many other children as well. At times there are over a hundred schoolchildren in Lichtentern, who are sometimes looked after by only two teachers. The cane is readily used. During the breaks, one of the children is often seen dashing to the fountain in front of the school-house to cool their fingers. Caning on the hand was a common method of punishment at that time.

Gertrud and Lina are accommodated in the "kinder-garten" in the morning. This is actually just a piece of fenced lawn so that the little ones can't get into the veg-etable and fruit garden and cause damage.

When spring comes, there is plenty of work for the children. The big garden has to be tilled, all the girls help with planting and sowing. Vegetables are at the top of the daily menu. There is stew day in, day out, always with the vegetables of the season. "Stew again!" is a frequently heard complaint.

Everything has to be grown by the community; even agriculture and livestock farming (with dairy cows and poultry) are practiced in Lichtenstern. The animals and the fields are mainly taken care of by the older boys, to-gether with state-assigned helpers from the Reich Labor Service. There is also a forestry office, because the woods around also have to be tended and maintained.

The girls have a lot to do in the garden. They line up in long rows to weed, sometimes singing a song. Or the auntie has them recite Bible verses by heart. Later, when it's time to harvest, the care workers have a clever trick up their sleeve, especially when it comes to picking berries. They have made a careful note of which girl doesn't like certain berries or fruits, and then she is the one chosen to pick them. That way more goes into the basket and less into the mouth.

"Actually I like just about everything, except Hutzel,"

says Liesl with a grin. But when she pops a handful of raspberries into her mouth, she sometimes gets a slap on the head. The aunties really do keep an eagle eye on everything.

Lina scurries around in front of everyone's feet, making a big fuss as always. She likes it in the garden, even if she is very clumsy when picking berries. If she is dismissed, she sneaks into the barn and strokes the cows. They hold very still, looking at her kindly with their big, gentle eyes. "Cow nice," whispers Lina.

A welcome change is offered by the annual summer festival, which in Lichtenstern involves elaborate preparations. The children can hardly wait, but first it's back to the hard work. Lined up on their knees, the girls scrub the big hall and clean the many small window panes so that the sun is reflected in them. The courtyard and garden also have to be tidied up and cleaned. After all, the guests from the surrounding area, especially those from the church organization, need to see that everything in Lichtenstern is kept in tip-top condition. In the kitchen, baking is busily in progress. The unfamiliar aroma reaches the children's noses, and they look forward to the treats: "Finally, cake again!"

On the great day, things really get busy. Tables and benches are set up in the courtyard, colorful paper flags are beckoning cheerfully. There is cake and juice for the guests, and also for the children. Plays and songs are performed and the children are mighty proud when the audience vigorously applauds.

The strange people are very friendly, and smilingly pat

the children's heads. A visitor wants to know from Lina whether they are always well-behaved. "Lina good, Gertrudle good too," she babbles cheerfully. She just loves the hustle and bustle and the attention. She is completely in her element and can hardly catch her breath. She beams at all the guests in a friendly way, and later waves goodbye to them.

To top it all, the visitors spread sweets on the children's beds: candy in colorful paper, cookies and even a few chocolate bars. What joy! But the aunties are again too quick for them, and in a jiffy gather up the sweets.

"Not all at once, each gets a piece today, and again tomorrow," Auntie Emma declares. Then she distributes the first chocolate bars.

Lina is still all fired up and licks her piece of chocolate with rapt attention. "Party again tomorrow?" she asks.

"No, silly," Auntie Emma laughs, "it only happens once a year."

Working is very important in Lichtenstern; slacking is frowned upon. Even in the evening hours there is no idle loafing, the girls have to knit or, more commonly, darn socks. Not a very popular activity. Lina can't help with this, handicrafts are completely impossible with her almost paralyzed hand. But she knows the song the girls made up about darning socks, and sings along loudly and correctly. She has long since learned it by heart.

Thimble on finger, stocking in hand,
we girls aren't too happy to sit in a band.

Darning and darning, day in and and day out,
to mend socks and stockings for small folks and great.
There are so many holes, as wide as a trap,
your darning egg falls through and lands in your lap.
So change your stockings, if the hole is still small,
we'll happily darn it and all will be well.

So the days go by and soon it is autumn again. Now the siblings have been in Lichtenstern for a whole year. There is always lots of work to do, as well as lots to learn, so the time has not seemed so long to them. The fruit harvest was exhausting and very productive this year. The children are happy when it is finally finished. In the evening it is already quite cold and it gets dark early. "Winter is calling," say the adults.

One morning at the end of November, Lina is washed particularly thoroughly. "Hold still now!" scolds Aunt Emma. "You have to be clean when the doctor examines you. Don't fidget like that and answer properly and slowly when he asks you something, do you understand me?" Lina nods, alarmed.

Aunt Sofie leads her into a room where the doctor is already waiting. He is very friendly to Lina and explains to her that he has come to Lichtenstern especially just to see how she is doing. Lina thinks that is very nice of him and she is happy, as always, when someone takes an interest in her. She immediately sings him her eternal party piece, "Comes a birdie a-flying", and counts to eight at top speed.

The doctor looks at Lina very carefully, from all sides,

so to speak. She even has to open her mouth. But she can't stand on one leg, especially not the right one. He also takes a close look at her "bad hand". Then he taps her back and monitors her heart with a listening device.

Lina is starting to get fidgety, she wants to go to Gertrudle: "She waiting," she tries to explain to the doctor. Aunt Sofie looks at her sternly and wags a disapproving finger.

Extract from the original report, dated 25 November 1930:

Findings: The child has something of a loving and affectionate nature, but she is also extremely restless, mercurial, and distractible.

She constantly wants something else, is always seeking attention, and disarms you with her sunny nature, which shows extreme joy when you are responsive. The child speaks a lot, hastily, very unclearly, sometimes quite incomprehensibly in her own word formations, and then again she can manage single, and even quite difficult words like "Gertrudle". She is very difficult and can be held still only for a moment at a time. Counts quickly to eight without a clear understanding of numbers. She can sing a song, accompanying it with gestures.

Physically: healthy, blooming, nice skin, hint of chicken breast, some lymphtomas on neck, slight goiter, narrow high palate. Right side of body somewhat paretic, musculature on right arm and leg flaccid and inferior to left, tendon reflex increased on right side. Heart and lungs in order. Assessment: Karoline clearly suffered a cerebral palsy very early on, the consequences of which are not only a weakening of the right side of the body but also a marked lack of inhibition in the emotional sphere.

In view of her extreme lack of concentration, the child can never be adequately accommodated in a normal school. And even if the intellect, which allows the child to absorb many passing things, were to be sufficient for a special school, the extreme psychomotor restlessness of the child does not allow her to be trained in such an institution. Thus the only option is to place her in Stetten or Mariaberg, and even there she will be hard to educate. The transfer can, of course, wait until next spring.

(signed) Dr. Koch

It's Christmas again, but this time the parents haven't come. Their father wrote in a letter that their mother was ill and they would have to postpone the visit until spring. But they have sent a package, a little something for each child: socks for Fritz and warm hats for the girls, plus a bit of Christmas cake. There is really nothing more to scrape together from the little they have left, but the children should at least be able to unwrap something at Christmas.

All over the country, food is becoming scarcer and poverty is steadily increasing. The economic situation in Germany is catastrophic, the number of unemployed rises to five million and things can hardly get worse. At

Lichtenstern, they are happy to be self-sufficient. Even though it's stew almost every day (known as "Lichtenstern Allround"), no one has to go hungry.

At Christmas, the children get a little meat and sausage, plus pastries and cakes. This is a welcome change from the unvarying diet. Each child receives a small gift from the home. Lina gets some colorful mittens, and finds them so beautiful that she doesn't want to take them off even indoors. Only when the aunties bring the dolls, which are only unwrapped in the Christmas season, does she quickly take off her gloves. The dolls' dresses have been sewn and knitted by the girls themselves.

In January 1931, Lina has to go to the Inspector's office. Aunt Sofie accompanies her. "So, you're Lina," the Inspector says solemnly, looking at her closely through his reading glasses. Lina feels uncomfortable and opens her eyes wide. The inspector laughs and says more kindly, "Don't worry, I won't hurt you." He asks all kinds of questions, which Aunt Sofie answers. He writes everything down exactly:

Original questionnaire for requests for the admission of
feeble-minded persons and epileptics:

Name, place of birth, date of birth of the person to be admitted:	*Karoline Bernhardt, born 02. 25.1924, Steinbach near Hall*
Name, status, profession, place of residence, religion of parents:	*Friedrich Bernhardt, casual worker, Protestant; Luise née Reber, Steinbach near Hall, Protestant*
Is the person to be admitted feeble-minded or epileptic:	*feeble-minded*
What is the person's mental state in general terms:	*mentally weak*
Where is the cause of the person's state to be sought:	*Cerebral inflammation*
What illnesses has the person already had:	*Measles, cerebral inflammation*
Is the person's physical development appropriate for the age?	*not notably handicapped*
Height:	*108 cm*
Weight:	*18 kg*
Are physical handicaps present:	*paralysis on the right side*
Does the person to be admitted have a conspicuous head formation:	*narrow shape of head, pointed at the top*
Can the person walk, and since when:	*yes, since age 3.5*

Is the person calm or constantly in movement:	*constantly in movement*
Does the person suffer from cramps:	*no*
Does the person have good vision and hearing:	*good vision and hearing*
Is the person's speech defective or good – since when:	*speech somewhat unclear*
Does the person speak words, sentences – ask and answer questions:	*asks and answers questions*
Does the person tell you all kinds of things:	*yes*
Does the person keep clean:	*yes*
Does the person drool from the mouth:	*no*
Any peculiarities:	*when walking, throws her head from side to side*
Can the person carry out small tasks:	*yes*
Feed him/herself:	*yes*
Dress him/herself:	*tries*
How does the person behave:	*comfortably*
Is the person good natured:	*very good natured*
Sociable:	*yes*

Does the person seek to be alone:	*no*
Does the person have the compulsion to break things:	*no*
Does the person hit or knock him/herself:	*no*
Does the person play? what with?:	*childish games, short attention span*
Is the child still capable of being educated:	*yes*

Lichtenstern, 19 January 1931, Lichtenstern Inspectorate

Finally Lina is allowed to rejoin the other children.

"What did the inspector ask you? What did he want from you?" Liesl excitedly asks Lina.

"Me not know, Lina good," she babbles impatiently and immediately runs out into the snow.

"Something is very wrong," Liesl says thoughtfully to Fritz. "They've got plans for Lina."

"Oh, what's the matter with you," her brother only replies, "after all she was so sick, no wonder they keep a special eye on her, what do you expect…"

Liesl has some idea what it is about, and she isn't happy about it at all.

Spring slowly comes on and the freezing nights are getting milder. This means that the temperatures in the old building are also getting a bit warmer. The parents have sent word and on a sunny Sunday in April they finally arrive.

Together they walk through the reviving monastery garden and sit down in the warm grass at the edge of the woods. They haven't brought Frieda with them, but the mother tells the children that they have another new little sister: "Her name is Johanna, but we call her Hanna."

The siblings are amazed. "Why didn't you bring her with you?" Liesl asks excitedly. "Of course we want to see her too …"

"Little sister?" says Lina questioningly, and snuggles up close to her mother.

"But that's not possible," she explains, "Hanna is only a few weeks old, we can't take her on a long train journey. She's at home with her aunt. Come now, Lina, just show me how fast you can run."

Lina doesn't need to be asked twice, and rushes down the hill at top speed together with Fritz and cousin August.

Liesl comes very close to Luise and whispers, "I think they have plans for Lina, maybe she will even have to leave this place. The day before yesterday they went through her clothes and thought about what she still needs …" She looks questioningly at her mother.

"You're right, Liesl," she says with a sigh, "Lina will probably have to go to Stetten, because that's where the children go who aren't quite 'right in the head'. Lina's not likely to get much better, so she can't stay here and she can't go to school either. In Stetten they have a special school for children like this. But don't say anything to Lina, she'll only get upset."

"But that's not possible!" Liesl is indignant and jumps

up. "She can't leave all by herself, she'll be scared! Gertrud and she always hang out together!" Liesl is quite beside herself.

Reassuringly, the mother puts her arm around her big daughter. "Oh Liesl, who knows, maybe things will get better soon. When the bad times have lasted long enough, better times will come around. Perhaps you will all be allowed to come home again one day."

Liesl gives her mother a look of disbelief, and silently shakes her head.

A cloud moves across the sun, and already the parents have to think about going home. Slowly and thoughtfully, they all walk toward the gate. At the gatehouse they stop for a while, and the father tells the boys about the locomotive that will take them home again. Luise takes each of her children in her arms once more and presses them briefly against her, only it takes her longer to say goodbye to Lina. She strokes her dark hair out of her face and says, "Lina, always be good and do what the aunties tell you, OK?" It costs her a lot to hold back the tears.

Lina, who is very sensitive to moods, at once notices that her mother is sad. Devoutly and quietly, she says, "Lina good, Mama not sad, OK?"

Luise finally tears herself away and waves to the children as they depart. Lina waves back enthusiastically.

Luise doesn't suspect that she will never see her special little Lina again in this life.

15 June 1931

Liesl and Fritz are taken out of the morning class by Aunt Emma. Astonished, they ask what is going on. The auntie only says that they must come along, they will find out in a moment.

At the gatehouse, Lina stands with a small cardboard suitcase. A big black car is waiting in front of the gate and a strange woman in a sister's uniform is just getting out. Lina looks quite lost and fidgets nervously; she is dressed particularly neatly, her dark braids carefully plaited. When she sees Liesl, she immediately runs to her and hugs her big sister.

Liesl's throat is dry and she can't get a word out. Fritz too looks quite distressed. Not even the car can distract him, though normally he can hardly contain himself when he spots a vehicle somewhere.

"Lina can now take a ride in the beautiful car," says the strange woman and smiles in a friendly way.

But Lina makes no move to part from Liesl. "Oh," she just says, and waggles her head.

"Come on, Lina, it's a long way to Stetten," Aunt Emma urges. She grabs the now crying girl and pulls her away from Liesl. "Now come on, you can go to school there too, I've already told you that," she adds to Lina, and has to swallow a few times herself.

"Stay, me!" Lina shrieks, outstretching her arms to Liesl. Her big sister is now also weeping.

"When will she be back?" Liesl asks, but the question remains unanswered.

"Let's go, you're only making it worse for the child. Say goodbye now," the strange woman urges and maneuvers Lina into the car.

"You must study hard, Lina, then you can come back to us soon!" Fritz shouts after her.

No sooner are the doors closed than they drive off. Stunned, Liesl and Fritz stand there and watch as the car drives down the hill. They wave until they can no longer see Lina's dark head.

"What on earth am I going to say to Gertrud?" Liesl sadly asks.

Stetten Sanatorium and Care Home in the Rems valley

With a jolt that travels right through her, Lina wakes up. Confused, she gropes for Gertrud, who usually lies next to her in the bed. She does not know what has happened to her or where she is. Slowly she realizes that she is in a car. She looks through the window, but it is dark outside. Quietly, she begins to cry again. She is confused, she is too hot and her throat hurts. "Don't cry, it's all right, sweetheart," she hears in a strange voice.

A hand reaches for her, and she is lifted out of the car and carried away. Lina no longer notices anything, she has fallen asleep and is once again dreaming of little children. Or maybe they are angels?

The first few days she has a fever and fantasizes a lot. She is taken to the infirmary and the nurses keep checking on her. Everyone hopes that the girl does not have something that is infectious.

Finally she has to go to the hospital, because her throat is swollen shut and there is a chance she might have diphtheria. But the X-ray shows nothing, no significant danger, her lungs are fine. She gets plenty of serum injections.

Slowly she is getting better. Once she becomes aware of her surroundings again, it is almost impossible to keep her in bed. Nervously, she fidgets around and keeps asking for Gertrudle and Liesl. The aunties and the sisters have a hard time keeping her calm. Auntie Berta finally succeeds by telling her stories and fairy tales about Liesl. All at once Lina finds she can lie still and listen.

By now it's the height of summer and Lina is allowed outside again for the first time. Only then does she see that she lives right next to a castle. She looks up at it in amazement, and also takes a good long look at the clock tower.

During a short walk, she flutters around everywhere like an excited butterfly. She darts here and there and everywhere, she wants to get a good look at everything. There's no stopping her, and the other girls from her section have to laugh at the funny new girl. Lina seems very happy and takes one girl after another by the hand.

"She's too happy for words," says Auntie Berta to her colleague with a laugh. "She'll settle in quickly here with her cheerful, sunny personality."

A description of the Sanatorium and Care Home for Feeble-Minded Persons and Epileptics, at Stetten in the Rem valley:

The institution was founded as a community of hand-icapped and non-handicapped people, and continued to be run in this way by the brilliant pedagogue and deeply religious Christian Johannes Landenberger in Schloss Stetten from 1863 on. His insights in the field of curative education have been incorporated into modern curative educational approaches. Inspector Ludwig Schlaich opened the special school in 1933, thus initiating the profession of curative education carer, which today, as a state-recognized specialist training, is largely responsible for the pedagogical support and care of mentally handicapped people. Today, the Ludwig Schlaich School of the Stetten Deaconry in Waiblingen also offers training courses in vocational and curative education.

(http://www.diakonie-stetten.de, accessed 06.12.2012)

The principal features of the extensive grounds are the castle and its garden. The girls' house, where Lina lives, is directly opposite the left wing of the castle. Right next to it is the school, and on the other side are the boys' house and a cottage hospital. There is also a playground, a castle garden and a beautiful big orchard. Further off there is farmland and a garden nursery, and various handicraft workshops are also located in the immediate vicinity.

Lina's father expresses his concern in a letter to Pastor Schlaich, Inspector of the Stetten Sanatorium and Care Home:

Esteemed Inspector,
Now that our child, Lina Bernhardt by name (a little girl), has been transferred from Lichtenstern to your institution, we would just like to ask how she is doing there. At the same time, we would also like to ask how long the train takes. Please tell us how far it is.
Friedrich Bernhardt,

Schwäbisch Hall, 07.05.1931

In Stetten, too, the daily routine follows exact and established structures. But unlike in Lichtenstern, everything is geared more to the needs and capabilities of the residents. In Lina's dormitory there are nowhere near as many beds as she is used to; only ten or eleven girls are accommodated in one ward.

Here, too, the day starts early. Children who need help washing and dressing are given it. Not only the aunties help, the older girls also have to lend a hand. Each one has "her child" to look after. The girls are very proud of this responsibility. So Anna helps Lina to get dressed and combs her hair.

"Come, come," Anna urges, "we don't want to be among the last to get to the dining room."

Lina gives her a warm hug and calls her "Liesl".

After breakfast and a short prayer, everyone goes back to their rooms. The beds have to be made, everyone has to try to do this for themselves and everyone is eager to do so. Then they wait for the ward visit. If this is delayed, they sing a little song to pass the time. Lina likes this and sings along right away without knowing the words.

The rounds take place twice a week. In addition to the doctors, the head of the institution, Pastor Schlaich, and the house father Mr. Herrmann take part. They greet each child with a handshake, which Lina likes a lot.

"So, Lina, you're feeling much better now, yes?" says the friendly pastor. "Now you can finally go to school, OK?"

She nods eagerly and immediately begins to count: "One, two, three, four …", following up at once with her favorite "Comes a birdie a-flying" and fluttering her arms. The gentlemen laugh loudly, and the aunties smile. Lina is happy.

At eight o'clock the school bell finally rings and the children can't be held back. Almost all of them love going to school. The lessons are seen primarily as entertainment, and as a welcome change from the routine. The different classes are not arranged according to age, but are geared to the abilities of the students. A lot of the work involves jigsaws, building games, songs and stories. Such things appeal to the children more than dry facts.

Lina is delighted with the school and with Miss Koch, her teacher. But she just can't sit still and clowns around a lot. The nice young teacher has trouble getting Lina to fit in. She always wants to be the first to do everything and simply can't hold back. Hitherto she has been indulged because she had been so ill, and she is also a completely new and unfamiliar face in Stetten. But Lina clearly has a tendency to push herself to the fore, even if she generally does it in a heartfelt and endearing way. This isn't going to be easy, the teacher thinks to herself.

At 9.30 there is a second breakfast during the long break. "It's unbelievable how hungry the children get! You'd think they haven't had anything to eat for weeks," says Auntie Berta to her colleague.

Lina loves the bread and jam. She definitely has a sweet tooth, and she licks her fingers with pleasure.

"How was school, Lina?" asks the auntie. "Do you want to go right back over, or would you rather stay here with me?"

"I have to go right back over, I need to go on studying," Lina answers very importantly. The aunties smile at her enthusiasm.

After lunch, the children have to rest. They put their heads on the tabletop, all in the same direction, so that none of the girls can get up to mischief with their table-mates. This doesn't suit Lina at all. Sitting still and being good for a whole hour at a time – not likely! Again and again she turns her head, makes some kind of disturbance or rocks back and forth on her chair …

"Lina, you must behave now," scolds Auntie Berta at last, "otherwise you'll be sent to the dormitory on your own."

"Back home we had a much, much bigger dormitory," Lina quickly retorts.

"That's enough now!" The auntie is really starting to get annoyed with the constant interruptions. "This is your last warning! And you've told us about the big dormitory often enough before."

Lina tries desperately to be good. But she doesn't find it easy.

In the afternoon, the children have handicraft lessons or gymnastics, depending on their capabilities and talents. At 4.00 they have coffee, and then finally it's time to play or go for a walk. Lina likes to be out and about, and she has quickly made two new friends. Hedwig is the same age as Lina and Helene (Lene for short) is two years older.

Arm in arm, the girls walk through the castle park while Lene tells fairy tales. "So a princess used to live in the castle?" Lina finally asks.

"I don't think so," Hedwig answers seriously, "otherwise she would have been feeble-minded as well."

Already they are being called for dinner. Hedwig is supposed to hand out the spoons today, so they hurry back to the large dining room. "What will it be today?" the girls ask themselves. Perhaps porridge, or cocoa and bread and butter? Or maybe soup with potatoes? On the occasions when apple tart is served, there is great enthusiasm.

After the evening meal, there is a short prayer. Most of the children have long been used to this and remain seated. Only Jakob gets up now and then and goes outside – some of them go with him. Lina, of course, also takes advantage of this opportunity; she doesn't want to sit still again.

It usually takes a while before the dormitories come to rest. It is not easy for the aunties to get the children to be quiet. Of course Lina is very wound up, especially during the early days in Stetten: she is always talking about the past day, there are just too many new things to excite her.

The past, her parents and her siblings, are almost quite forgotten. Only shortly before falling asleep does she sometimes ask about Gertrudle and Liesl. The auntie just answers, "They are safe in God's hand, just like you, my child." The evening prayer finally calms her down enough for her to fall asleep.

So the summer passes. As expected, Lina has settled in quickly and easily. The institution in Stetten is now her home, but of course she knows that she actually comes from Steinbach near Hall. However, these are only words to her; they no longer have any meaning. Lichtenstern, especially the big dormitory and the garden, still surfaces in her memory from time to time.

She now has to learn to write with her left hand, and also to knit – both of which are far from easy for her. The teacher has to come up with a lot of ideas to keep the girl on side. But Lina is good-natured after all, and when she is complimented, she continues to make an effort. She loves to learn songs, and the aunties are often amazed when Lina sings them the song she learned in the morning faultlessly in the afternoon. Songs, melodies and music are what she likes best.

When they go out for a walk, children now need to wrap up warmly. Summer is finally over. Dressing is always quite a hassle, often the girls mix up all the clothes and even lose track of shoes. It can actually happen that they put on shoes that don't match. Nevertheless, they march merrily along, following the motto, "What doesn't fit can be made to fit." The shoes are always cleaned immediately, and they are supposed to do the job themselves.

Each child is given a daily task in the house. This "assignment" is taken very seriously and they always do their best. Lina is proud when she is allowed to help with something, just like the other children. But she can't hold back: she always wants to be the first to have her "assignment" given her and pushes herself forward, which is not appreciated. Lina has to learn to fit in. This is very difficult for her at first.

One day she is assigned her task last and stubbornly

refuses to do anything at all today. "Everyone comes last once in a while," Auntie Berta explains to her calmly, "and if you don't learn and realize that, I'll just have to punish you. Then there'll be no cake for you tonight."

Lina is horrified, because all day the children look forward to the cake. She quickly grabs the broom and starts sweeping. "I'll do it, I'm good again, please, please not punish."

Auntie Berta is satisfied: "That's right," she says and strokes Lina's hair. Lina is beaming again - she is never sad for long, but almost always sunny and content. This is confirmed by the following report:

Short Report, 17 September 1931

Lina seems to be quite happy here. In terms of conduct, she does not make any special effort. Pre-class 1 with Miss Koch. Outwardly seems quite bright and mentally alert, but actually is rather weak. She has a good memory for songs (melody and lyrics).

Christmas 1931

Weeks before Christmas, a magic settles over the entire institution; everyone is eagerly awaiting Christmas Eve. All the residents and staff agree that Christmas in Stetten is something special. The whole castle shines in a special light. Long before Christmas, many packages and parcels arrive, which are immediately "taken care of" and stowed away out of sight.

On Christmas Eve, a play is performed in the girls' house. The children have been rehearsing with their teachers for a long time and everyone is very excited. Lina is actually allowed to be an angel, something she has wanted for a long time. She excitedly "flutters" around in her beautiful dress. She's even got wings, but sadly they get stuck at once in the door frame.

"So, angel, now you can't fly anymore," grins Elfriede, one of the girls, enjoying Lina's discomfiture.

Little Inge looks up at Lina with wide eyes and says, "Angels don't always have to be able to fly. You are beautiful, Lina."

Lina beams, and says, "Right, I'm a proper angel all the same."

"Well, yes," Auntie Berta says, putting her head on one side, "most of the time anyway."

After the performance of the play, it's time for the presents and finally the door to the castle's large dining room opens. Several big fir trees are standing there, shining and sparkling. Almost two hundred people are gathered today, there's quite an uproar. There is a gift at every seat, but they are not allowed to be unwrapped just yet. A real test of patience begins, because first the Christmas story is read, then everyone sings a few Christmas carols together.

Lina suddenly becomes thoughtful: Christmas last year comes back to her mind. She remembers her siblings and also, very dimly, her parents and the aunties in Lichtenstern. Furtively she looks around and sees that some children, and also a few adults are crying. They must feel the same way, they too think of their relatives and of home.

No sooner has the last carol been sung than everyone rushes to get their presents. "Open it, open it!" is heard on all sides. Lina is distracted from her gloomy thoughts and quite skillfully unwraps her package. Oh, what a joy: "A storybook and in color," she cries excitedly, "that's just what I wished for from the Christ Child!" Of course, she also has to marvel at the other presents – there are all kinds of tin and wooden toys, trumpets and drums, practical things like clothes and even a whole ham sausage.

Pastor Schlaich and his wife have also come, they look around with interest and share the happiness of those who have received gifts.

For the evening meal there is cocoa and white bread, which everyone likes. Afterwards there is a service. The chapel is almost bursting at the seams today and is beautifully decorated. Before going to bed, the parcels that the children have received from home are distributed in the girls' house. The aunties want to make it easier for those who have not received anything from home, so they give them out late in the evening.

Lina's parents have also sent a gift. Full of joy, she unwraps two chemises with her name embroidered on them.

"Well, your mother has done a beautiful job there," says Auntie Berta admiringly, "and look, a little card with an angel on it, it says: *To you, dear Lina, we wish a Merry Christmas and hope you are well. From your parents.*"

Lina's eyes again fill with tears.

"Now, now," says the auntie, "let's not have any more crying, now that you've got such pretty things. It's time for prayers, and then a nice sleep." Quietly she turns out the light.

That Christmas Eve, Lina dreams of home for the first time: her father holds her in his arms and her mother strokes her hair. Her brothers and sisters are also there: Liesl, Fritz, Gertrud, little Emil and two other very small girls whose names Lina can no longer remember. The strange thing about the dream is that no one is laughing or even smiling.

Pictures of Stetten and Lichtenstern

School in Stetten (Stetten Archives)

Children at Stetten, Lina probably on left
(Stetten Archives)

Lichtenstern

Dining room at Lichtenstern

1932 and 1933

In February 1932, Lina is mentioned in a report to the State Welfare Authority in Stuttgart. She is described as follows: "A dear child, perhaps a bit superficial, but still full of warm fellow-feeling." Her concentration difficulties are also mentioned. "She is content with her life on the Schlossberg. Everyday life in Stetten does not cause her any problems, and she is also enjoying school more and more."

When it gets warmer, she is outside on the playground every free minute. She has made friends with many girls and also likes to play with the boys. She drives little Karl around for hours in the handcart, until eventually he complains, "Hey, I am allowed to get out, right?" Lina promptly drives him back to the boys' house and waits there for new passengers.

Lina finds housework and handicrafts less entertaining. Although she wants to be involved in everything and to be up front, she still can't work well with her right hand because of the paralysis. The aunties, the nurse and the doctor show her again and again how she can use her hand a little, but Lina is rather stubborn and doesn't want to. She has gotten used to her disability, and prefers to do everything with her left hand.

The aunties and all the adult residents of the nursing home often talk about Adolf Hitler, Soon everything will be different, they say. The name comes up again and again. Lina says to her friend: "Adolf lives in the boys' house too, doesn't he?"

"Oh, you are a silly," Hedwig replies. "Adolf Hitler, he's not a boy, he's the Chancellor."

"Whatever is that?" Lina asks, impressed.

"Oh, something like a king or an emperor," says Hedwig, who is not particularly interested.

"OK, but we live in a castle too. Come on, let's play princesses again," is Lina's answer.

This gives the girls more important things to do. Hedwig can make beautiful wreaths out of flowers, and the two princesses then walk with them through "their" castle garden.

In Stetten the political changes do not stand out much at first, even though the state capital, Stuttgart, is only 15 kilometers away. Occasionally you see men in brown uniforms, and even children seem to follow this trend. The red swastika flag is waving in some places; sometimes people make the Hitler salute.

Life in the sanatorium and nursing home goes on as usual, people live as if in their own little world on the Schlossberg. There is enough to do every day to keep the residents happy. During the summer, everyone who can do anything at all is busily at work. Even the smallest ones are eager to help with berry and fruit picking. Most are proud to be able to help, only a few refuse to work. Some are just physically unable to do so.

In July another letter from Lisa's parents reaches Stetten:

Hall, 15 July 1932

Dear House Father Herrmann,
We would just like to ask you how Lina is doing.
Especially if she is making progress with her studies
and is in good health. We have been wanting to come
for a visit, but the bad times do not allow us. I don't
have any work either, though thank God we are still
healthy, which we also hope for Lina and the whole
institution. With warmest greetings from the Bern-
hardt family.
Lots of love to Lina.

In response Inspector Schlaich writes a letter to Lina's
parents:

Dear Mrs. Bernhardt,
Since our "missionary" is on vacation, I will give you
a short report about Lina. She has been in our pre-
class for a year now.
She is quite lively, has learned many expressions and
also memorizes things relatively easily. She is quite mu-
sical and is not unskilled in mimicking, doing puzzles
and building. Above all, she has learned one thing
at school this year: how to fit into an orderly system.
However, we do not have high hopes that she will ever
learn much. She is still not always clean, but otherwise
does not make any particular trouble in her section.
She would probably be very happy to receive a visit.
Yours sincerely,
Inspector Schlaich, Stetten in Remstal, 21 July 1932

"Your parents send their love and ask you how you are doing at school," Auntie Berta tells her.

Lina is amazed: "Father and mother … When are they coming to visit and bring little sister with them?" she asks thoughtfully. Somewhere at the back of her mind, her parents take on a hazy shape. More clearly, she sees the siblings in front of her, standing at the gate and waving goodbye. "How are Liesl, Fritz and Gertrud?" Lina suddenly asks.

Auntie Berta is astonished by the clearly formulated question and by the seriousness of the child. "They are fine, don't you worry about them."

Lina nods absently and goes back to her work. Today it's her turn to hand out plates, and she has to be careful not to drop a single one. Even if the plates are only made of tin, she would be embarrassed. When she's finished, Auntie Berta praises her: "You've done a great job, you're already a big girl," she says affectionately and gives the beaming Lina a quick hug.

The rest of the year passes placidly and without any major events. At Christmas Lina receives another gift from her parents: a woolen scarf. In the enclosed letter, they explain that it is the best they can do and they are happy if they can send each child at least a little something. A beautiful Christmas card arrives from Liesl. She reports that Fritz often misbehaves and has to be punished. Also Cousin August "is not doing well", she writes, he has already run away twice …

Lina is now nine years old, and mostly happy and content. She knows her way around Stetten quite well by this time, and is allowed to run small errands occasionally. She proudly walks around the grounds with her basket, and of course has to tell everyone what she has to do. So it can happen that she is out and about for quite a long time, as she is easily distracted by everything and everyone. As long as she shows up on time for meals, the aunties have no problem with it. "Well, Lina, have you had a few chats again?" they say good-naturedly. "Oh yes, the cobbler's cat has had kittens," she reports enthusiastically, "I just couldn't get away."

Lina loves animals and regrets that she is not allowed to bring some kittens onto the ward, but the aunties are strict on this point, it is not possible. There are some semi-feral cats in the castle garden, and some of them let Lina pet them. She likes little children just as much, she is always happy to mother them …

"Auntie Berta, I had a dream last night," she says one sunny spring morning. There was a little boy who was crying so much that I said, 'You don't have to cry so much, I'll be with you soon and can hold you in my arms.' Then he smiled at me. That was my little brother, right? The one who is with the dear Savior?"

Auntie Berta suddenly feels cold, despite the spring sun. "Come on, Lina, today you can try to get dressed all by yourself," she says quickly to distract the girl.

Lina has been suffering from a sore throat for a long time. It just won't get better on its own. Finally she is taken to the hospital and has an operation on her tonsils. This is not uncommon in the Bernhardt family. Almost all of her sisters have been through this operation.

In the hospital, she cries a lot. The only way to keep her quiet is by reading stories. When she returns to Stetten, she enthusiastically tells the other children about the ice cream she was allowed after the operation.

In early 1933 another report is sent to the State Welfare Authority:

Deportment: sometimes a bit self-willed, but generally sweet-natured, easily guided, has also become cleaner. Little progress. Will never be able to work or be released from the institution. Palatal and one pharyngeal tonsil removed, otherwise physically healthy. Intelligence age 5, intelligence quotient 0.55. Special schooling to continue despite the child's mental weakness, since the father is a drinker and the child cannot be released into his household.

At this time, negotiations about her further placement begin. Her father tries everything in his power to bring Lina home. Again and again he writes to Inspector Schlaich, and expresses himself to the same effect at a court hearing.

Extract from the transcript of the negotiations with the Welfare Education Committee of the Württemberg State Welfare Authority:

The child would come under section 73 of the RJWG [Reich Youth Welfare Act], according to which the welfare education authority can release a minor on the grounds of impracticability of welfare education if he or she suffers from hereditary, mental or psychological irregularities. The Youth Welfare Office of Hall first heard the father's views on this question. "I won't leave the child in care education any longer, and demand that she be returned to my household. The child's imbecility is not so bad, it would be fine to take him home." The father sticks by this statement. Bernhardt, who is known as a drinker and is also without gainful employment, lives with his wife and a two-year-old child in a room in the poorhouse (Hall Municipal Hospital). The Youth Welfare Office observed that neither the external circumstances nor the behavior of Mr. and Mrs. Bernhardt had improved significantly and that returning the child to their household would be unacceptable.

On 21 July 1933 the Welfare Authority writes to the Stetten institution as follows:

The Hall Youth Welfare Office cannot approve a leave of absence for the girl, because the parents' living conditions do not support it and the parents cannot provide the desired assurance that the child will return to the institution without serious prejudice. Under these circumstances, we ask that the girl's leave of absence not be granted.

Lina doesn't hear anything about all these doings; she is content to live her everyday life in Stetten with all its joys and sorrows. Now and then she is a bit stubborn.

Knitting, for instance, she doesn't like at all, in spite of repeated encouragement to keep on trying. Then she uses her "poor hand", to get the sympathy of the others and to be excused the disagreeable task. If that doesn't help, she has been known to hurl the knitting into the corner. Her pronunciation is also often criticized; she is always being told to speak more slowly and clearly. She can't pronounce the "KR" sound at all. Lina doesn't say "It was crazy" but "I wa razy". Now and again she makes an effort and pronounces the words almost correctly, but mostly she forgets and babbles wildly unchecked.

She prefers running around outside and playing with her many friends. This is actually quite in the spirit of Inspector Ludwig Schlaich, who repeatedly points out how important it is for the disabled to feel comfortable in their surroundings. This, he says, brings them on them more than one might think, and games and sports should not be neglected either. In his opinion, regular daily routines are essential, because they provide security and have a healing effect.

Auntie Berta's report (1933) paints a vivid picture of Lina:

Karoline Bernhardt, nine years old, is one of the younger children in the section. However, she has a great need for recognition, which manifests itself in the fact that she likes to push herself forward. She also tries to attract attention with her gestures. At times she plays with the other children, e.g. in the circle game; she actually joins in with real devotion.

When she feels uncomfortable, her behavior is very childish, and she draws attention to herself to an exaggerated degree. She doesn't often do things on her own. Washing and dressing she is capable of only to a limited extent. If she is given a warning, she obeys at once; but after a while she reverts, so the after-effect does not last long. She seems completely unconcerned a short time later. Caressing other children is a routine thing with her. Already after some time she uses the phrases and expressions of adults.

1934

The boys in Stetten are suddenly all playing soldiers and are only interested in tanks and fighter planes. "They're crazy," say the girls scornfully, who would rather play weddings and princesses. Finally they come to an agreement and play war and peace alternately.

April 20 is a holiday, there is even cake and cocoa. "Because it's the Führer's birthday," Fritz shouts loudly so all can hear. Most of the children don't really care. The main thing is that it's a cake day and they are let off school.

Meanwhile, the negotiations about Lina continue. The State Youth Physician speaks of releasing her from the institution, since the goal of welfare education can never be achieved (whatever that goal may be). At the same time, however, the father should be denied custody. Furthermore, it is pointed out that she cannot be released until the application for sterilization has been filed and decided upon.

Already on January 1 1934, a Law for the Prevention of Hereditary Diseases has come into force. This provides for the sterilization or "rendering infertile" of persons with alleged "hereditary disabilities". In 1935, a Law for the Protection of the Hereditary Health of the German People was enacted. In October 1934, a Dr. Eyrich from Stuttgart contacts the management in Stetten with an application for infertility treatment.

Dr. Eyrich's original letter, dated 11 October 1934:

To the Management of the Sanatorium and Care Home, Stetten in Remstal

In the enclosures, I am submitting an application for the rendering infertile of Karoline Bernhardt, with the request to attach an expert opinion by the head physician of your institution and to send both to the competent hereditary health court in Schwäbisch Hall.

In my letter of 9.4.34, I naturally assumed that the District Welfare Office was also of the opinion that feeble-minded persons in need of institutional care, for whom the goal of welfare education is not attainable, should be left in the institutions at the expense of the welfare of minors in cases where, as here, the domestic circumstances obviously do not ensure sufficient protection, until the prospective Reich Preservation Law comes into force, in order to prevent worse things from happening.

First of all, what has been achieved so far on the girl will be lost in a short time. Hence previous expenses will have been in vain. Sooner or later, however, the feeble-minded girl will have to be taken into care again, only in a considerably less favorable condition than at present, or she will become a burden to the public in some other way — a carrier of venereal diseases together with the necessary treatments, other hospital stays, begging and the like, police costs, etc. - costs which, according to all experience, are higher than those of keeping her in an institution. The serious moral danger that such a girl represents for the rest of the youth will not be touched on here, as it cannot be calculated. I do not have the competence to make an application for the withdrawal of custody. This would be a matter for the District Welfare Office. Incidentally, nothing in the Law for the Prevention of Hereditary Diseases stands in the way of the child's being released from the institution. In this respect I must correct my expert opinion of 9.4.34. The child, who is only 10 years old, cannot be considered a reproductively capable person with an inherited disability.

Medical Councilor Dr. (signed Eyrich)

"Well, that's a pretty abominable production," says the Stetten doctor, shocked.

The sister, who knows Lina well from her hospital stays, shakes her head angrily: "What these high and mighty gentlemen in Stuttgart think up with their unbelievable laws. They make the little innocent girl look like a criminal, it's outrageous!"

"Be careful what you say, they're the ones in the driver's seat," the doctor cautions and puts the letter in Lina's file.

In all this "to-do", the angry letter from Lina's father goes almost unnoticed.

Original letter, 11 October 1934:

*To the Sanatorium and Care Home, Stetten in the
Rems Valley*
*Have received your letter and taken detailed note
of its contents. I am sorry not to be able to share
your opinion on the matter in question concerning
my daughter Lina.*
*It is not possible for me to comprehend why a child
who is physically and mentally very retarded should
be subjected to sterilization at this stage. I think I
may assume that the time for this sterilization will
have come only when my daughter has reached sexual
maturity. To the best of my knowledge, such sterilization may not be performed and I ask that my point of
view on the matter be communicated to the court. It
is inexplicable to me that the Youth Physician should
have made an application to this effect to the State
Welfare Authority, since it was precisely this authority that had advised me to hand over my daughter
to your nursing home. It would be much better and
more in the German spirit if I were to be told in no
uncertain terms: You can't have your daughter, for
this or that reason. I therefore ask you to inform me
in good time of the date on which my daughter will
be leaving, so that I can collect her from you.*
Patriotic German greetings, Friedrich Bernhardt

Anyway, Lina remains in Stetten; that's where her home
is now. Only occasionally, when the other children come

back from vacation and talk about their homes, does she become thoughtful. Often she then starts to tell them – something or other. "But that's not true," Auntie Berta says sternly, "you're making things up again." Sometimes Lina herself can no longer distinguish between her invented stories and the truth.

Her dreams also often get her all confused. She often greets the auntie in the morning with: "I dreamt something again …" Once she says: "Last night I had a dream about you, Auntie Berta. The two of us were driving in a big beautiful car – all the way to my mother's house, she's had another little girl, that's my little sister Elsa." Again and again, the aunties are amazed at the imaginative stories that Lina tells. Most them involved children, and often babies as well.

The caregivers talk about it. "Maybe she misses her brothers and sisters more than you might think," says Auntie Berta. "It's a pity that she doesn't get at least one visit, she would be so happy about that."

Her colleague nods: "Yes, but the siblings are also in a children's home, and the parents certainly don't have the money for the train fare."

In Stetten, too, there is an annual festival in the summer, which is no less cheerful than in Lichtenstern. The festival begins with a morning church service. In a report, Lina's attitude to religion is described as follows:

I asked Lina why we go to church, to which she replied: "Because it's a church service and we must not forget the good God." She speaks with a lot of feeling of the poor, dear baby Jesus, and of the dear Savior who was crucified.

After church there is food and singing, and many different games are played. Lina is all fired up again with joy and walks through the castle park with her friends. There are booths and tables set up everywhere. "Everything is so beautifully colorful," Hedwig says, delighted. If only it could always be like this.

In the evening, the children are so tired that they almost have to skip washing. Totally exhausted, they fall into their beds and dream of the beautiful day they have had.

But everyday life resumes again much too soon.

In a report by the caregivers (aunties), we read the following about Lina:

Lina's memory for songs is excellent. It is hard to say what it is like for stories and experiences, since she adds all sorts of poetry when recounting them. She has a very active imagination, and since she loves listening to stories, this indicates intellectual interest. Lina is also very plaintive, and tries to gain the pity of the aunties in every way possible. She always expresses her wishes in a pushy manner.

She is very lively during games and sports, and when out walking she is interested in everything she sees. Lina makes up to the caregiver at every opportunity and she is also very attentive and kind to her fellow inmates. For example, she immediately notices when a button is missing from a piece of clothing. If one of the children is sick, she shows him her compassion in an exaggerated way. Lina is always cheerful and happy; I have never seen her in a depressed mood for long. She never takes anything without asking, nor does she lie. She is very happy when she can make others happy. If the children want to do something good for Auntie, she is always on board. But if they want to do something mean, Lina may well say, "You mustn't do that, or Auntie will be sad." If Lina has done something wrong and needs to be punished, she gets so scared that it is almost impossible to carry out the sentence. If you praise her, she always tries even harder to do her best.

Lina is now no longer the youngest in her section, and she is allowed to look after little Margarete. She is very happy about this and cares for the girl lovingly. "Marga, you're my baby now," she says proudly, taking the little girl by the hand on a walk.

"Oh, look, there's an airplane, a fighter plane!" Willi suddenly shouts and all the children stare spellbound into the sky. "Is Adolf Hitler flying in it?" asks little Schorschi. Willi shrugs his shoulders. Lina is still staring at the sky. The airplane is already no more than a speck.

"But Lina, where is your little girl?" asks Auntie Beate suddenly.

"Oh!" Lina is startled and runs off. Where has little Marga gotten to? Oh, there she is, standing under a tree …

"Now that gave you a fright," says Auntie Beate. "You must always keep an eye on Margarete and not get distracted all the time."

Lina nods silently and looks down abashed, at the same time holding Marga's hand tightly.

At school, Lina suddenly has vision problems. Again and again, she squeezes her eyes tightly shut and complains, "Can't see." Finally, the teacher talks to the house father. "Lina has something wrong with her eyes, she needs to see an ophthalmologist," he tells the Inspector.

And sure enough, on a cool morning in November, Auntie Berta says to Lina: "So, you're not going to school today, Auntie Beate is taking you to Stuttgart to see the eye doctor."

"No, no, not to the doctor, don't want to!" Lina screams right away. She remembers her last hospital stay, somehow it is always associated with pain when she has to do with doctors.

"But you silly goose, it doesn't hurt at all. You can take the train and Auntie Beate will buy you something good to eat on the way. You'll like that, believe me."

Beate, who is still young, looks forward to the trip to the city: "Yes, Lina, you'll see, this will be a nice day for us." Finally, Lina is helped into her coat and they set off for the train station.

The train ride is very exciting for Lina, she is glued to the window and has her mouth open in amazement. "Now don't get sick," warns Auntie Beate with concern.

When they arrive in Stuttgart, Lina's eyes are like saucers: "So many people and beautiful cars and these huge buildings – just look, Auntie Beate!" she calls excitedly. "Yes, that's what it's like in a big city," Beate explains.

Finally they reach the ophthalmologist's practice. Lina immediately wants to hide behind Auntie Beate – the white coats scare her. "Don't worry, little lady," the doctor says kindly, "you just have to look through this apparatus. That's all, it won't hurt at all, I promise, and there'll be a surprise for you afterwards."

Indeed the examination is quite painless. Lina dutifully looks into the device – sometimes with her left eye, sometimes with her right, as the doctor tells her. He turns a few screws and cogs, murmurs something under his breath, and it's over. "You've done a fine job there," he says, "and now you get your surprise."

Lina looks with fascination at the shimmering green glass marble that the doctor has given her. "Oh thank you, doctor, I've never seen one like that before, they are the most most beautiful ones," she stammers with emotion. "The spectacles will be ready in two weeks," the doctor tells Auntie Beate.

And here they are on the street again. "So, Lina, let's eat a pretzel first. I need a coffee and you need a lemonade," Beate says cheerfully and takes Lina by the hand. "Come on, Madame, let's find a nice café." The two of them set off, beaming. What a beautiful time they are having.

Back in Stetten, Lina talks for days about her trip to the big city. Of course, she also shows everyone her beautiful marble. Enviously, Hedwig thinks she too is badly in need of glasses and must urgently visit the eye doctor.

When the glasses finally arrive, it takes some time for Lina to get used to them. At first they make her feel dizzy, and she is also always leaving them lying around. The aunties scold her a lot, explain how expensive such spectacles are and tell her she should be happy and grateful. Eventually her eyes get used to them and she sees everything wonderfully clearly.

The forgotten family – 1937

The days and weeks pass by in relatively regular courses. Holidays, celebrations and birthdays provide a welcome change from the routine. Lina is still quite content with her life, she seems basically cheerful and balanced. Only rarely does she draw unpleasant attention to herself. But she seems to have become a bit more thoughtful, for instance when other children are allowed to go home on vacation or get visits from relatives. Her dreams probably also change during this time.

One morning, Lina says, "You know, I don't have anyone anymore," to which the auntie vigorously replies, "But Lina, whatever are you talking about? You have a big family and lots of brothers and sisters. And you have all of us here in Stetten, too." "But I dreamed I was all alone in an empty room, and I was so afraid." "Oh, child, that was just a bad dream," the auntie quickly consoles her.

One Sunday in August, Lina is sitting in the sandpit with Karlchen, baking a cake. Suddenly Auntie Berta comes running and gasps breathlessly: "Lina, there you are! I've been looking for you everywhere. Just think who is here to visit you!"

"Someone to visit me?" asks Lina with amazement, getting up quickly.

"Yes, just imagine, your father is there and your aunt. Quick, brush the sand off your hands and come with me, they are waiting for you in the hall."

Lina trots slowly along behind Auntie Berta. She understands what it means to have visitors, but it has never happened to her here before …

A big dark-haired man with a mustache is waiting in the hall. He is wearing a dark suit, but without a collar or a pocket square. A small older woman stands next to him. She looks a bit strange – something seems to be wrong with her mouth.

"Well, Lina, at last I get to see you again," the man says and starts to walk toward her. He notices how astonished Lina is and adds, "Say, you don't even know who I am."

Lina just shakes her head silently. Unusually shy, she tries to hide behind Auntie Berta.

"Now come, Lina," says Bertha, "you're not a baby anymore. Your father and aunt have specially come such a long way to see you, you can shake hands with them both." She pushes Lina forward. "Well, she's just a bit shy at first. Hmm, Lina?"

"You've grown into such a big girl," the father marvels. "How old are you now?" asks the strange aunt.

Lina just shrugs her shoulders, she's not so good with numbers, she can never remember them. "Lina's thirteen now," Auntie Berta puts in.

They sit down at a table. Auntie Berta fetches tea and some bread and jam for the travelers. The two gratefully take some and talk to the auntie. Lina sits next to them and listens intently.

"It's really tough the way things are these days," the father begins, "we've wanted to come and visit Lina for so long, but it just wasn't financially possible for us. It is a long journey from Schwäbisch Hall to here. My wife couldn't come with us, she's in the hospital."

"Oh, I'm sorry to hear that. What is the matter with her?" asks Auntie Berta.

"Well, you know," sighs the father, "it was all the grief with the children. Now they've taken the three little ones away too. My wife was so upset that she hit the bottle, and I had to take her to the hospital. There was no alternative. Now she has to stay there until next year."

"God will give her the strength to get through it," says Auntie Berta quietly.

"You know, we just don't have a chance anymore," says the father, "they're constantly targeting us. I was in the war, and always tried to do right by everyone. But their lordships think they are the leaders, and a poor, penniless citizen has no say in the matter." Suddenly he grins and continues: "The other day we were visited by a guy from the town hall, a snooty ass from the party. We were just about to have lunch. My wife said: 'So, first we must say grace.' I was surprised, because she never does that. But this was a special prayer, it went like this: *Come, Adolf Hitler, be our guest and give us what you promised us. Not just a crust and a scrap of herring, but what you eat along with Göring. Amen.*"

Auntie Berta holds her hand over her mouth and snorts loudly. She quickly looks around to see if anyone else is in the room.

"That popinjay from the town hall went off like a bat out of hell," laughs the father, "he turned bright red and slammed the door on his way out. My wife has an implacable hatred for this whole gang, and no wonder. All this nonsense with the race laws: since when is someone with dark hair worth less than a fair haired guy? That's outrageous! We are all real Germans. During the war, no one asked me about the color of my hair, I was OK as I was."

"What are the other children doing, the older ones?" Auntie Berta says, creating a diversion. She is not entirely comfortable with such speeches; you have to be careful what you say.

"Liesl found a situation with a baker's family in Heilbronn," the father reports, "she liked it there. She also visited me a few times in Hall. We were glad that she had landed on her feet. But then an accident happened."

"What was that?" asks Auntie Berta.

"Liesl was waxing the stairs with liquid wax, when somehow it all caught fire and she got burned really badly. The poor girl is in the hospital now and is completely swaddled in bandages. Her life is no longer in danger, but it's not easy for the poor kid. There will surely be scars and other infirmities left behind. Such a young girl, it's a bad lookout for her. The doctor has forbidden her to be given a mirror. This week I have to go back and check on her."

"Oh dear, that is truly a misfortune, especially for such a young pretty girl." Auntie Berta shakes her head sadly.

"And Fritz, now, he's going to work for a farmer just outside Hall. I'm glad he's staying close by. Gertrud and Friedel are in Lichtenstern, we visit them often, it's not that far," says Lina's father to conclude.

"Gertrud keeps asking for you, Lina," he says, turning to his daughter. "Gertrudle," Lina says devoutly. "Yes, that's right, you still remember her," the father smiles and strokes Lina's hair. "The three little children are in the children's home near here, we'll stop by there later, too. It's not easy," the father sighs, "but I'm glad that Anna helps me around the house. She's my cousin," he explains. "She's always been given a hard time of it, because of your cleft palate, haven't you Anna?" Anna just nods her head sadly.

"Why don't you take Lina for a bit of a walk," Auntie Berta suggests. "Lina, you can show the visitors around, take them to the school and the girls' house – what do you think?"

Lina is immediately thrilled. It is terribly important to have visitors, after all, and by now she has thawed out a bit.

She eagerly shows her father and the strange auntie around, and is soon chattering away. She introduces her visitors to everyone they meet. "They've come a long way to visit me," she explains importantly. Finally, they walk through the sunlit castle park, her father with his arm around Lina.

"You don't even know that you have a new baby sister and baby brother," says the father. "Their names are Elsa and August, and they're still quite small," he says.

"Yes, I know," cries Lina quickly, "I dreamed about Elsa!"

"But that's just not possible," says her father - "somebody must have told you."

"No, that's not true," Lina stubbornly insists, "and I often dream about the little brother who died. Tell me again what they're all called, please!"

Her father has to think about it, and starts hesitantly: "First Liesl, then Fritz, then you – no, wait, Karl, who died, and then you; Gertrud, Emil, Frida, Hanna, Elsa and August. Ten children and none of them are at home with me anymore," he murmurs sadly under his breath. Lina reaches for his hand and squeezes it. "I'd love to take you with me," he says with a smile, "I could use a big girl like you at home, you could help me a lot. I'm sure you're a very industrious child." Lina nods eagerly.

"Oh, I haven't told you yet what Gertrud got up to in Lichtenstern," says the father with a grin. "Just imagine, she got so mad at Auntie Sofie that she put thumbtacks under her cushion. When the Auntie sat down on the chair, she immediately jumped up because they were all poking her in the butt."

Lina practically doubles up with laughter. "Gertrudle so funny," she yelps excitedly. "But you mustn't do that," she then quickly adds.

"Of course not, and the auntie was pretty angry too. At first she didn't know who had done it. That's why she said that the annual outing for all the children would be canceled if the guilty party didn't come forward. That was too much for Gertrud – she didn't want that either, so she owned up. Of course she got a beating, but at least she was allowed to go on the trip," grins the father.

"Oh, that must have hurt Gertrudle – but also the auntie," says Lina and has to laugh again.

Lina shows them the girls' house, the school and, of course, the castle as well. By now it's well into the afternoon, and the father looks up at the clock tower. "It's almost four o'clock, we have to go, because we still want to visit the three little ones in Waiblingen. We can't just turn up under cover of darkness. The drive home will take long enough."

"Oh, I want to come too," Lina exclaims and clings tightly to her father's arm.

"That wouldn't do," he says, "we've got to get back directly from there to Hall."

"Yes, it's a long journey on the train," Anna speaks up for once. "But we'll talk to your Auntie Berta and see if she won't let you go to Waiblingen one day to see your brothers and sisters."

"So, Lina, now we have to say goodbye," says her father, when they are standing by the gatehouse again.

In the meantime, he and Anna have spoken to Auntie Berta. She said that she would ask the Inspector to allow Lina to visit the three siblings. Of course, she couldn't make the decision herself, but since the children's home is only a few kilometers away, she thinks it will certainly be possible.

Lina's father looks very unhappy. He hugs his daughter for a long time. Auntie Anna strokes her head and murmurs something about God's blessing.

"Will you come again soon?" asks Lina.

"That won't be so easy," her father answers, "but we will see if we can come to your confirmation. And perhaps they will actually let you come home soon, I'm not giving up hope. When your mother gets out of hospital and is feeling better, there won't be any reason why not."

Lina's doesn't quite understand this – home, for her, is here in Stetten. But she doesn't say anything.

"I would so much have liked to take you with me right away," the father says sadly. "But you be good now and don't forget all of us."

Then again Lina is standing there and waving – until she can't see the two figures anymore.

Auntie Berta keeps her promise and talks to the Inspector. And indeed, Lina is allowed to visit her siblings in Waiblingen. Of course she is very excited and looks forward to the break from routine. Every day she asks when it will finally be the day of the visit.

At last the day arrives and Lina travels with Auntie Beate to the children's home. A woman in a stiff sister's uniform leads them through the building, past a room with small white beds. This is where the youngest children sleep.

"Oh, so many little children," Lina marvels. She stops curiously at a window, and looks with enthusiasm into a room where there are many baby cribs.

"Come on now," says the nurse, and takes Lina by the shoulders, "your sisters are in the other room, with the older children. Your brother has already been taken in by a couple from A., he's not here anymore."

"Oh, oh," Lina says and waggles her head back and forth with excitement.

The woman looks her earnestly in the face. "Do you understand at all what I'm saying to you?" she asks forcefully. Then shaking her head, she says to Beate, "The girl isn't right in the head, is she? She's feeble-minded. What a waste of effort!" she adds coldly.

Beate replies, visibly furious: "We'd like to see the two Bernhardt girls now, if you don't mind. Nothing else needs to concern you."

They enter a large room where there are several children. Some are playing with wooden blocks and plates; that's all the toys there are. The nurse grabs a girl about six years old with rat tails and a defiant look on her face. "So, this is Johanna," she says gruffly, setting the child down in front of Beate and Lina. Then she pulls over a smaller girl with dark hair and big fearful eyes: "And this is Elsa. There you are," she adds icily, and hurries off.

At first, the three of them eye each other suspiciously, but then Lina kneels down to the two frightened children and whispers with them. Beate also joins them and says kindly, "So, you two, this is Lina, your big sister." At once Lina grabs both of them and clutches them against her. "Little sisters," she says tenderly. Beate warns her not to be too violent: "They have no idea who you are, you'll only scare them."

"Let go!" Hanna is already complaining, and frees herself from Lina's embrace. Elsa doesn't seem to mind; she puts her finger in her mouth and looks up at Lina with interest. Finally, the siblings play with the few building blocks; Lina tries to build a tower for them.

Hanna asks, "Where is Papa?" Lina shrugs her shoulders. "Foo, foo," Elsa interrupts loudly. "She wants something to eat," Hanna explains. That's when Beate remembers the cake she packed. It is quickly distributed and just as quickly devoured. The girls lick their little fingers and Elsa beams at Beate. "Are you staying here now?" asks Hanna hopefully. "No, no … we have to go again, the bus is leaving soon," Beate says sadly. "But I can't leave them here with the evil woman," Lina says in horror, pressing the girls to her again. This time they don't resist. Elsa leans comfortably against Lina, and Hanna also puts up with her caresses. It almost breaks Beate's heart to see the siblings like this.

At the end of the room, an elderly woman is sitting and knitting. Beate talks to her a bit, and is quite relieved when she tells her: "The two girls won't stay here much longer. Two families have already offered to take them. It's a pity they can't stay together, but anything is better than this." Beate nods silently, feeling infinitely sorry for all the children here.

"We have to go," she says to Lina when it's time to leave. "Please start to make your goodbyes. But you don't need to worry about them, they will soon be taken in by some nice people. They'll be fine then, believe you me."

Lina nods calmly, and quickly presses a kiss on each sister's cheek. The two stand silently side by side and look sad. Beate wonders if it was such a good idea to bring Lina here – when she has to leave again right away.

"Life is not fair," she murmurs softly to herself.

On the way home, Lina asks, "Why was the woman so mean to me? Just because I'm a bit slow? And what is feeble-minded?"

Beate sighs: "Some people are just mean, and very easily influenced as well." Lina looks at her questioningly, she didn't understand that at all. "*Feeble-minded* is a stupid word. We prefer to say *handicapped*, and that just means, as you said yourself, that you learn a little slower than others."

Both thoughtful, they arrive back in Stetten and everyone is surprised that Lina, contrary to her usual way, says hardly anything about the visit to her sisters.

"Wasn't it nice at the children's home?" Auntie Berta asks in surprise. Lina just shakes her head peevishly. Beate tells her colleague about the visit and adds, "I didn't feel good about it at all. It's just not right to tear a family apart like that."

Dark times – 1938

Lina in no way corresponds to the ideal image of the "German girl" and the time in which she lives could not possibly be more hostile to her.

In 1933, she was still certified as having an IQ of 55, which corresponds to a mild mental handicap. In subsequent reports, the tone becomes increasingly harsh and the IQ is suddenly downgraded to 45, approximating to a moderate intellectual deficiency.

Lina's file, however, does not contain a single IQ test. The reports about her are generally somewhat confusing and apparently contradictory. On the one hand she is said to have a vivid fantasy, but then again there is talk about limited imagination.

14 April 1938

To the District Welfare Office, Schwäbisch Hall
Dr. Gm./L.
Re: care of minors with reference to Karoline Bernhardt, born 25.02.1924, Hall-Steinbach
Karoline Bernhardt is a feeble-minded girl with an intelligence level of 45, i.e. her mental condition is such that it may be said in advance that one can never expect average performance from her, it will always be below average. She has always been a sweet child, somewhat superficial, with poor imagination and concentration, and has made little progress in school. So the question of her learning a profession can

The fact that she can't write with her right hand has suddenly also become a problem. "A German girl writes with her right hand," is current doctrine. Lina has practiced so laboriously with her left hand and can now produce quite neatly written sentences, as a handwriting sample in the file shows. Now, all of a sudden, this is no longer thought to be correct.

Even her having dark hair, as many of her family do, is suddenly seen has an inferior trait. "The fair-haired guys are the officers," Karlchen orders, when the children again go marching in the castle courtyard. "That's a stupid game," the girls complain. "We're not going to play any more."

Lina's friends of the same age are now called upon to do "useful" work. If possible, they should learn a trade so that they can "earn their own bread one day". In Lina's case, they think long and hard about where they could send her, in which craft workshop on the castle grounds she might be useful. Especially because of her right hand, the possibilities are very limited. For now, everything remains the same and she continues going to school.

Dr. Eyrich had already filed an application for "sterilization" in October 1934. He had been somewhat hasty there, as Lina was only ten at the time. But now she is 14 years old and the "period of grace" is definitely past.

"Today we're going to Waiblingen again," Auntie Beate announces to her one morning in September.

"To the little sisters?" asks Lina, astonished. She immediately realizes that this can't be the case: "But they were taken in by good people."

Beate does not explain: "Come on, get dressed quickly. No, not your everyday clothes, put on your beautiful new dress."

Lina is a little confused, but the prospect of an outing and a car ride soon makes her forget to be concerned.

Finally she is sitting in the car next to the auntie. Beate has a large bag with her and makes an uncomfortable face.

"What's in there, and where are we going now?" asks Lina impatiently.

"You'll see soon enough," is the curt reply.

The car stops in front of a large building. Lina is already starting to shake as they walk through the entrance. "No, no, not to the hospital, I'm fine, I'm healthy!" she cries in panic and clings tightly to Beate. She remembers earlier hospital stays and the pain they caused all too well. Already she is being held by two nurses and Auntie Beate has disappeared. "Beate, Beate, stay! Don't leave me here!" screams Lina. Beate runs out the front door and covers her ears.

In the car, she gives vent to her grief: "I really don't know if I can or want to go on," she sobs. "It's just not right to torture the poor girl like this. What is the point of it all?"

The driver replies sullenly, "It's a good job they're making the idiots infertile, there are enough of them after all."

Unfortunately, more and more people in Germany have been of this opinion ever since Hitler had his dream of the "Aryan man". The German people should no longer be threatened with "contamination" of their genetic make-up, they must be bred to be superior through targeted "selection", according to the racist ideology of the National Socialists. On propaganda posters, disabled or mentally ill people are depicted as "useless eaters" and as a threat. Sayings like "Anyone sick is a burden" and "Only the strong shall survive" are widespread. Physically or mentally handicapped people are classified as "unworthy lives", and everything that does not fit into the world view of the National Socialists is to be "eradicated".

Lina is sedated for the time being. The senior consultant, Dr. Pröhlmann, then examines her quickly, but Lina is unaware of what is going on.

A common method of compulsory sterilization at that time is the removal of the ovaries, which of course requires general anesthesia. When Lina slowly wakes up the next day, she realizes that she is not lying in her bed in Stetten, but in the hospital. Everything hurts her, and she also feels terribly sick from the drugs. She cries silently to herself, her whole abdomen burns like fire. She can't understand what has been done to her. She was healthy, wasn't she? Again and again she calls for Beate or Auntie Berta. The nurses give her something to calm her down; after all, they have other things to do and can't keep looking after the "little simpleton".

Everything was done as had been ordered:

State Health Department, Schwäbisch Hall – 29.08.1938
To the Management of the Sanatorium and Care Home, Stetten in Remstal
Re Karoline Bernhardt, born 02.25.1924 in Hall-Steinbach
In the case of Karoline Bernhardt, an order for sterilization was already issued by the Hall Genetic Health Court on 20 Oct. 1934, on grounds of congenital imbecility. This decision could however not be carried out at the time because Karoline Bernhardt had not yet passed the age of 14. Now that she has reached this age, I request that this procedure be carried out within 14 days. I enclose the certificate of legal effect with the request to return it. I also ask you to send me the medical reports on the sterilization when it has been performed.
The Department Physician (signature not legible)

Here is the succinct response from Stetten to the letter of 08.29.1938:

Re Karoline Bernhardt
Returning herewith the certificate of legal effect of the decision, we beg to inform you that Karoline Bern-

hardt was sterilized at the Waiblingen Hospital in the period from September 6 to 19, 1938.

Lina is still struggling with pain and loneliness in the hospital. She is quite in awe of the nurses anyway, and hardly dares to speak to them.

At last Beate comes to visit, bringing clean clothes and a few apples. Lina is delighted, and wants to pack her things to go home right away.

"No, Lina, you need to stay here for a while, the scars have to heal properly first," Beate tells her.

Once again Lina asks: "What am I doing here? What did they operate for? I wasn't sick at all." She had been unable to get an answer from the hospital staff. Be good and pipe down – that was all they had to say.

"There was something that needed to be fixed in your stomach, you wouldn't understand," is Beate's evasive response.

Dr. Pröhlmann had answered in a similar way, to which Lina said: "I was fine before – but I'm not fine now!" The doctor told her not to be cheeky.

Beate has to leave again directly. "I'll come soon to take you home properly, you just have to wait a little bit longer," she promises.

Lina is gradually feeling better and begins to be bored. She keeps getting on the nurses' nerves with her complaints; no one has time for her here. In the bed next to her is a little girl who has had an operation on her tonsils. Susi cries and cries and whines for her Mommy. Now Lina has a job to distract her. For hours she sits by the little girl's bedside, and comfortingly strokes her hand. Eventually, the child calms down and finally falls asleep. "That's nice that you're looking after the girl," says the unbending nurse, pleased. "Who'd have thought that you would be good for something after all," she adds coolly.

Lina is not discouraged. She tells little Susi about Elsa and Hanna, her little sisters: "They too are all alone with strange people." Susi is impressed and forgets to cry.

In the afternoon, Susi's mother comes to visit, which is a joy. Susi doesn't want to let go of her at all. Finally, she whispers in her ear: "Lina is always nice to me."

Immediately the woman thanks Lina: "That's very sweet of you to look after my little one. She's never been away from home, so she is afraid here in the hospital." Lina just nods, she understands that very well.

The next day, Susi's mother brings sweets and a big colorful book. "There, now you girls have something to look at," she says kindly and divides the treats between Lina and Susi.

Lina is thrilled, especially by the storybook. She can't really read, she can only piece together a few short words. But the pictures are enough to fire her imagination; she makes up her own stories. Susi listens with great interest. The two of them are so absorbed that they don't even notice when the doctors come by on their rounds. Only when Dr. Pröhlmann stops at Lina's bedside and yanks the blanket away from her do they look up, startled.

"Well, that looks pretty good," he says with a glance at the scar on her lower abdomen. Lina stares at him darkly.

She doesn't like this man who always treats her as if she were not there. "She can go home tomorrow," he says. This, however, makes Lina very happy and she beams – finally. "Heil Hitler," the doctor salutes as he leaves the room. Lina covertly sticks her tongue out at him. Only Susi has seen it and starts to giggle.

Next day the girls say goodbye to each other. Susi is also soon going to be allowed to go home. "I'll visit you in Stetten," she promises. Her mother nods and shakes Lina's hand. "Yes, Lina, we live not far away from the castle in Stetten, we'll visit you very soon, that's a promise."

"You see," says Beate as she leaves the hospital with Lina, "now you've actually made new friends and will soon have visitors, so the hospital stay was worth it after all."

Finally back home, Lina thinks, as they arrive in Stetten. Although she still doesn't understand what happened to her in the hospital, she tries not to think about it anymore.

Her friend Marga is 18 years old and knows a lot, especially about men and women and all that. "They fixed it so you can't have children," she explains to Lina bluntly. "The Fuhrer decided that must be done with all the idiots. They did it to me a long time ago." "Yes, but children come from the good Lord – and only if you are married," Lina says seriously.

"Oh sure, I suppose you still believe in Santa Claus and the Easter Bunny, too." Marga takes Lina's arm. "Come on, let's go for a walk and I'll explain a few things to you."

So Lina gets a vivid account of the facts of life. Shaking her head, she listens to Marga, not quite believing her, but somehow it does sounds logical. Lina decides to keep it all to herself for now.

In the evening, she is very depressed and seems visibly unhappy, so that Auntie Beate asks what is wrong with her. "It's just a pity, that I'll never be a mother," Lina says softly and hugs her doll. Auntie Beate is so shocked that she doesn't know what to say.

Later, Beate talks to her colleague about it: "Lina knows a whole lot more than you think. I wouldn't have thought she knew what has been done to her."

"Yes, you're right – she's very observant about a lot of things," confirms Berta. "It's good that Christmas is coming soon. It's a good way to distract her, even if she no longer believes in Santa Claus."

A few weeks later, in November 1938, synagogues are burning down all over Germany. Jewish stores are demolished, daubed with slogans and looted. Jews are taken from their homes, mistreated, arrested or killed. Their belongings are confiscated.

At this time, the residents of the Stetten institution have no idea that they are in the path of an avalanche.

1939/40

Popular enthusiasm for Adolf Hitler continues, and the call for war does not die down even in the spring of 1939. Hitler speaks about the conquest of new living space: the German people must be able to expand.

In September it finally happens, and German troops invade Poland. Living space to the east is rapidly occupied. The armed forces are self-confident and sure of victory: "Today Poland belongs to us, tomorrow the whole world." The war has become a reality.

In Stetten, too, enthusiasm knows no bounds; the management staff of the institution are fully behind the Führer. Propaganda films about Adolf Hitler are shown in the gymnasium. Lina finds the Führer rather frightening.

"Why does he have to scream like that?" she asks. She doesn't understand what he is screaming about. "But he doesn't look like a nice person," she remarks.

"Hush," Horst reprimands her, "you mustn't say anything bad about the Führer!"

The songs and the marching music, on the other hand, are much more to Lisa's liking. She claps her hands enthusiastically with the others and joins in the singing.

At Christmas 1939, Lina's parents write another letter:

Esteemed Inspector,
Unfortunately we could not take Lina on vacation,
because it was impossible for us to get the money for

the trip. We will send her something later. Would you be so good and write us if Lina will be confirmed this spring. We would like to come to that. We might then be able to take Lina with us if the institution allows a vacation. We hope Lina and all of you are well. Respectfully, the Bernhardt family

"We're having a party on New Year's Eve," Marga whispers to Lina, "I've collected a few treats and Willi has hidden some schnapps." Lina's eyes widen. Marga is always talking about Willi, whom she meets secretly. "And this time you're coming too," Marga quickly adds. Lina is not entirely comfortable with this, but she is curious.

On New Year's Eve, there is stew with sausage – a delicacy, when lately the sausage and meat rations are constantly being reduced or even altogether absent. The children enthusiastically fish all the pieces of meat out of the pot.

Right after dinner a few of the girls, including Lina, sneak off following Marga. They quickly run through the castle park and over to the nursery garden. Willi and two of his buddies are already waiting at the tool shed. Horst, known as Horstle, is also there. Lina knows him well. She likes him because he is always sunny and cheerful.

In the tool shed, the young people hunker down on fruit crates and sacks. Marga has all kinds of Christmas cookies and even a sausage. Wherever did she get all this from? They help themselves with enthusiasm.

Willi passes the schnapps bottle around. Lina just

smells it and shakes her head in disgust. "Come on, don't be a wimp," Horstle says kindly and puts his arm around Lina. She bravely takes a small sip and immediately has to cough terribly. The others all laugh. "That's our baby," says Marga equably.

Lina is rather uncomfortable with all this, and says anxiously, "But it isn't allowed, we must go back to the girls' house or Auntie will give us a telling off."

"Now don't be a wimp," says Horstle again and squeezes her even more tightly.

"Let go, I want to go to Auntie Beate!" cries Lina. "First you'll have to give me a kiss," is his answer.

The others laugh and clap their hands. "Lina and Horstle, Lina and Horstle … kiss, kiss!" they sing with abandon. Lina tries to resist, but Horstle is stronger and finally presses his lips to her mouth. This is wet and unpleasant, but the others are thrilled and applaud. Marga and Willi also kiss, long and hard.

When Horstle reaches for the schnapps bottle, Lina seizes the opportunity, jumps up and runs out of the shed. She quickly gets back to the girls' house in the darkness. She is in luck. In the general New Year's Eve hustle and bustle, no one has noticed that a couple of girls are gone.

A few days later, Marga has disappeared. Lina searches the entire castle grounds for her. Perhaps she has had another secret tryst with Willi. Finally, she asks Auntie Berta. "Marga has been transferred to another institution," Berta tells her, "and it's better that way. Such a lot of trouble she made with the boys!"

Lina is not sad for long; she has many other girl friends and the new year brings quite a few changes. Sometimes she sees Horstle and waves to him. He always waves back with a smile.

"Horstle is nice, I'll marry him one day. Then we'll both stay here at the castle with you for always, Auntie Berta, right?"

"Oh, my goodness, child," laughs the auntie, "let's hope not. When you grow up, I'm sure you'll find a good position."

This is exactly the question currently being considered at the institution. On February 25, Lina will celebrate her 16th birthday. Normally, girls of this age are placed in positions, for example with farmers. Of course, only if they are suitable. Otherwise, they are placed in a trade within the home. With Lina it is difficult to find anything suitable. Due to the paralysis in her right hand, she is not much help. Finally, she is assigned to the institution's own weaving school. She likes going there and is eager to "help", but she doesn't manage to do much. Nevertheless, everyone there likes her. With her imaginative stories, she provides welcome distraction and keeps them amused.

Lina attends confirmation classes for a few weeks and eagerly learns Bible verses. Memorizing is not difficult for her, and at services in church she recites almost everything correctly. Sadly, confirmation is a small, modest affair. The girls get new dresses and are spruced up for the occasion. Lina's parents did not come, but she did not expect them to. The aunties did not mention to her that her parents had been invited, to spare her the disappointment. So like the others she is happy with her new dress and the cake in the afternoon.

Inspector Schlaich and the doctor have volunteered for the war. They are soon called up, and will be back only occasionally on leave. In the doctor's place, a lady doctor has been appointed: Dr. Leonie Fürst. Lina is completely enchanted by the nice, young, good-looking doctor. At last she doesn't get a turn anymore when she sees a white coat.

Original letter of 15 May 1940 to the District Welfare Office, Schwäbisch Hall:

Re: care of minors with reference to Karoline Bern-hardt As we already informed you in a report to the State Welfare Authority of 02.20.1933, the subject will never be capable of working or of being dis-charged from the institution.
Today's report by the sanatorium doctor reads as fol-lows: Short-sighted girl, paralyzed on the right side, cannot comb her own hair, make her own bed, etc. Knits with difficulty. So cannot be considered for a rural service position.
Karoline was confirmed this spring. It was not possi-ble for us to place her in one of our workshops or to get her a place to learn domestic tasks and skills. We send her to our weaving school, where our physically and mentally weak inmates are kept busy with light work. She occupies herself in the weavery with plug knit-

ting and yarn winding. She also offers to cut up old garments, but even this she cannot manage, although she tries hard.

On the ward, we have got her to the point where she is capable of dressing herself and helping to dress smaller fellow inmates. For other work she lacks understanding and physical strength.

Karoline Bernhardt is a sweet and friendly girl who causes no trouble for her carers. She is also well liked at the weaving school. In our opinion, it is impossible to place Karoline in service on a farm. Whereas we can only accustom her very slowly and in a modest compass to light work here in the institution, she would certainly be more of a burden than a relief for a family outside. We believe that it is advisable to wait and see how the skills of the girl can be developed and furthered in our weaving school. Whether it will be possible at some point in the future to transfer Karoline to an institution for part time workers is something we are not able to judge at this time.

Stetten in Remstal

l:v: FR (Fürst)

In the meantime, things have become unbearably crowded. The institution for epileptics in Korb has been closed, and all residents have been moved to Stetten. Lina is not too much put out by the tense situation or the overcrowding. She is friendly to all the "newbies" and is happy when she can show someone the way or help them out. She watched the arrival of almost 400 people with interest and wondered where they would all be accommodated. Several rooms were commandeered in the school building, and the gymnasium had to be used to house the new arrivals. And two additional beds have been squeezed into Lina's room.

The new residents from Korb have a hard time finding their way around in the strange surroundings, and so it is quite unsettled in Stetten. Food is also in short supply: "More water in the soup," is the order of the day in the kitchen. Nevertheless, the housekeeping staff in Stetten are proud that no one has to go hungry. The aunties and caregivers hardly get a moment's rest either, and are stretched to their limits every day. But everyday life in the institution somehow goes on, and everyone tries to make the best of the things.

In the afternoons, Lina now helps in the weaving school. Mainly, she unravels old pieces of clothing and rewinds the wool. "Did I do a good job?" she keeps asking the supervisor. "Yes, Lina, it looks pretty neat. You're really trying hard today, but I can't be checking on you every five minutes." As she passes, she strokes Lina's hair.

There is a lot to do in the weavery, especially now that everything is in short supply. All funds have been greatly reduced. Germany needs its money for more important things, and the "idiot institutions" are put on the back burner. "The Führer has ordered it this way, because the war and the soldiers are the most important things now. Every good German should be happy to make sacrifices," Lina and her friends have been told. "What is the war for? What do we need it for?" the girls ask. "The people need new living space, and it is there in the east. The German Reich should be able to expand," is the sort of thing they are told. "I don't want to go to the east, I'd rather stay here in Stetten, I know my way around here," Lina declares. The aunties laugh fit to burst.

On a beautiful spring day in May, Lina is sitting in the yard with her friend Lene. The two are enjoying the warm rays of sunshine. "Look, a tour bus!" exclaims Lene, pointing to the portal. "Maybe we'll finally be allowed to go on a trip again!"

Indeed two gray buses have appeared by the gate. A few men get out and walk across the castle courtyard to the management offices.

"No, I don't think we'll be getting a ride," Lina observes.

Some of the former residents from Korb are to be picked up. But since no one has been informed beforehand, it takes several hours to get them ready to travel.

"So where are these people being moved to?" the caregivers ask. They have a hard time getting together the people on the list at such short notice. Of course they assume that the intention is to relieve the overcrowding at Stetten. Nonetheless, there is general restlessness and confusion.

"Why do they of all people get to go on a trip?" grumbles Lene. "They haven't even been here for long!"

"Well," Lina replies, "they're going to live somewhere else so it won't be so crowded for us here." The girls watch the people getting in, and wave to them.

Lina overhears two men who have arrived with the bus talking. Grinning, one of them says, "Soon that will be 70 mongrels less." They laugh and then also get on board.

Lina is puzzled. She doesn't understand. Mongrels are dogs, she is clear about that. But what do dogs have to do with it?

The beginning of the end

It's the start of summer 1940, and Lina and her friends are still enjoying life outdoors. They happily go for a walk and let the boys tell them about the latest war events. They remain unimpressed, as the boys brag about German triumphs and the blitzkrieg in France.

Lina goes happily to the weavery and puts in a lot of effort there. Every girl who is at all capable knits socks and gloves for the brave soldiers at the front. Pictures of the Führer are now hanging on the walls everywhere and the red flag with the swastika flutters at almost every window.

One day there is great excitement, when the Inspector comes to Stetten with his troop. They stay overnight in the institution. He and his comrades are given a grand welcome. There is a slide show and a thanksgiving service in the chapel for the successful French campaign.

Lina has a tryst with Horstle behind the greenhouse in the evening. The tool shed burned down just the other night – probably others were using it as a hiding place where they could smoke in secret.

When Horst tries to kiss her again, Lina jumps up crossly and shouts, "No, that's not allowed, or else they'll send me away too, just like Marga!"

"Did she get taken away in a gray car?" asks Horstle. "The ones that get picked up that way don't live for much longer," he adds.

"Whatever you say, I don't believe a word of it, you

just want to frighten me." Lina doesn't find this funny anymore.

Horstle however will not be diverted. "But I heard someone say – the mongrels are all being gassed!"

Lina jumps up. "We're not mongrels, we're people!" she cries. Horstle just shrugs his shoulders, disturbed. Both of them stand around, somewhat distressed.

"I dreamt about my little sisters again today," Lina finally says. "They were both dressed up and going for a walk, and our parents were there too – they went to a pub and drank lemonade. Elsa had a big ribbon in her hair and Hanna had really nice, new shoes. They both waved and shouted that I should come too. But suddenly there was a ditch and then there was fog as well, and I couldn't see them anymore."

Horstle takes Lina's hand and says, "Come on, there are some lilies of the valley blooming, we can pick a bunch for Auntie Berta."

Auntie Berta is delighted with the fragrant flowers that Lina brings her. "But wash your hands well, Lina, because the flowers are very poisonous." Lina obeys, but says thoughtfully, "Why are such beautiful flowers poisonous then, and how can people be mongrels at the same time?" Berta doesn't understand the meaning of the last question, and she has too much to do to think about it for much longer.

Everyday life in Stetten goes on as usual; not much has changed on the Schlossberg yet. Even the annual festival is celebrated – but on a small scale, without too much hustle and bustle. Several fathers and brothers have gone to war, which in most cases the relatives make a big thing about. The field postcards are taken everywhere and shown around at every opportunity. No one believes that their loved ones will stay away for long – the heroes will surely return home soon, after winning their battles. The disgrace of the First World War finally seems to be a thing of the past.

The summer goes by much too quickly. On a Tuesday in September, Lina comes home from school. There are a surprisingly large number of people moving around on the courtyard, and the atmosphere is quite tense.

"Look there, Lina!" Helene calls and points to the gate. The girls stare wide-eyed at the two gray buses waiting there. The Inspector and Dr. Leonie are standing next to them, talking to some strangers. "I'll call the ministry first!" Lina hears the Inspector's agitated voice.

The young lady doctor continues to negotiate with the visitors, finally hurrying across the courtyard to the Inspector's office with some papers in her hand. Lina and Helene have meanwhile taken refuge in the dining room; all they get is a hasty soup. Some girls and women are missing from the table, and everyone is very restless. What with all the excitement, the soup goes cold. "Come on, let's go back out and see what's going on," Lina says to Helene.

At first everything is calm, but Lina has a bad feeling when she looks at the buses. She thinks of Horstle's words and says urgently to Helene: "No matter what happens, don't ever get on a bus like that!"

"Why not?" asks Helene. "You're usually the first to volunteer for an outing."

Then suddenly a commotion breaks out. The sisters and aunties appear with some women, most of them carrying a bundle of clothes. "You're just going to another care home," the aunties keep saying soothingly, but some women cry and scream, clinging to the carers and refusing to get in. They struggle and scream and rave. Others get on the buses waving happily and one says, "So, we get to go for a ride." There is quite a scramble.

By now Lina has fled to hide under a staircase. "Don't get on!" she wants to scream, but she is completely rigid. Everything suddenly happens very quickly. Hardly have the women boarded the buses, and now all Lina can see is the dust thrown up by the vehicles as they turned on the courtyard.

She remains sitting under the stairs for a while. She hears the inspector and Dr. Fürst in a loud an animated exchange. Then, eventually, everything falls quiet.

In the evening, Lina naturally asks the aunties where the women have gone and when they will be back. But she doesn't get any sense out of them. "To another institution, in Grafeneck. We'll just have to see …" they say evasively. Apparently they don't know the meaning of today's happenings either. Lina at last falls exhausted into a troubled sleep.

In the morning, she again has a dream to report: "My sisters were there, but all five of them, and we were playing nicely together in the sunshine. Then a big boy came and stood blocking the sun. He said, *Lina, don't ever get on a gray bus, or you'll be killed, too!* That was my big brother, he knows everything."

"Now Lina, don't talk such nonsense," scolds the auntie, "you'll drive everyone crazy with your stories." But somehow the auntie's voice is trembling and she looks quite scared too.

Just three days later, disaster strikes yet again. This time, 60 male residents are taken away. Lina doesn't notice much this time, because she is in the weavery, and no one is summoned from there. But she certainly notices the panic and horror that prevails everywhere in the evening. The peace and quiet in Stetten is finally over. Rumors of killing centers, which had been circulating for some time, began to take shape. There is sheer horror and also an inability to believe it. The caregivers cannot and do not want to imagine what could have happened to their charges. They still try to explain to the residents that they have been transferred to other institutions. But when the first death notices of the "transferred" inmates arrive, no one believes them anymore.

"The Grafeneck home in the Swabian Alp has become a murder factory," whispers one orderly to another, "and there are several such extermination facilities in the country; the useless eaters are all being gassed."

When the gray buses show up at the gate again on September 18, the residents are in mortal fear. Some have taken refuge and cannot be found. Others thought they would be left alone because their names had been crossed off the lists the previous time. Now they are on the list again. They have to be dragged to the buses, flailing wildly.

Lina has again taken refuge under the stairs. She

watches in terror the gruesome spectacle as it unfolds. Suddenly she can no longer suppress a scream; her friend Helene has just been pushed onto the bus. Lina bites her hand and cries softly to herself. Everywhere people are wailing and fighting back in vain. Some try to escape and are caught again. The carers, and Dr. Leonie as well, try their utmost to calm the people down, but there is no chance of their succeeding. They themselves seem to be at the end of their tether.

Late in the evening, when her hunger gets the better of her, Lina crawls out from under the stairs and sneaks up to the girls' house. Auntie Berta silently takes her in her arms and holds her close for a long time, then she brings her warm milk and a piece of white bread.

"Where is Helene?" asks Lina quietly. The auntie just shakes her head silently and cannot hide her tears. In bed, Lina tries to pray as the auntie has told her to. Above all, she asks God to bring Helene back and to take care of all the other poor people, because they can't find their way around, they've only ever been here in Stetten.

In the home, nothing is as it once was. Many residents are missing and entire rooms are empty. The management of the institution is considering how the vacant space could be used. A retirement home is being discussed – negotiations are underway with the authorities in Stuttgart.

Death notices of the "transferred" patients now arrive almost daily; the causes of death stated are quite implausible and seem impossible in the light of their medical histories, which are well known to the staff. It is clear now what the "transfers" are all about. "Gassings, that's what it is, it's mass murder!" an enraged carer exclaims. He is promptly summoned by the management of the institution, who make it crystal clear to him that he is signing his own death warrant by making such statements: "Just keep quiet, otherwise your name will be on the list next time!"

The extermination facilities are no longer a secret. Some parts of the population, including the church, take offense. The home at Grafeneck in the Swabian Alp is closed soon after. This is where most of the Stetten inmates have died.

Every time a car engine is heard, panic breaks out among the remaining residents. Lina immediately rushes to hide under the stairs. She still hopes that Helene might come back after all. But Horstle has explained to her that this is impossible – no one will come back. "Hermann was lucky, he was on a trip with his aunt when they came to pick him up – otherwise he would have been gone too. And Hans goes on a long trip to his relatives every Tuesday, because the buses always come on Tuesdays," says Horstle. "If only someone would pick me up," he sighs, but he hardly has any relatives left.

Lina has also thought about this – her distant and almost forgotten family comes to her mind. For a long time there have been no letters or parcels. "Your father must be in the war, and your mother is often ill, isn't she? Maybe she's in hospital again," Auntie Berta says, searching for an explanation.

Actually, Lina doesn't want to leave; she has always

liked it in Stetten and it's the only life she knows. But recent events have taken a terrible toll on her. The constant unease and the nightmares every night make it very difficult for her. She always dreams of the buses and also of Helene, who desperately calls out to her. She wakes up almost every night screaming and drenched in sweat.

Just for a brief period, everything is quiet in Stetten. On Tuesday, November 5, Lina sits with Horstle once again behind the greenhouse. They are a bit cold, but Horstle has organized a piece of plaited bun from somewhere, and they eat it with enjoyment. Horstle puts his arm around Lina and says, "It's warmer like this, right? I don't think we need to be afraid anymore. There haven't been any buses for almost two weeks, they've killed enough of us now."

"I don't know, I'm still afraid, Lina whispers.

Today, Lina and Horst don't hear the buses arrive. The nursery is too far away. They sit peacefully together and think about how the coming Christmas will be, now that everything has changed so much.

Suddenly an orderly is standing in front of them, and they both jump up, startled. "Oh, there you are," he says to Horst in a friendly way. "Come with me, my boy, I have something to show you."

Lina trots curiously along behind. In the courtyard, she stops, frozen with fright. The orderly has grabbed Horstle by the collar and is dragging him to the buses by the gate. There he is handed over to a couple of men. Loudly Horstle screams for help, shrieking that he doesn't want to die: "I'm not really an idiot, I can manage just fine! Help, help!" But already he has been pushed into the bus.

Lina stands in the middle of the courtyard and screams like a banshee, completely beside herself. First Helene and now Horstle, it's too much, she can't stop screaming. Finally Auntie Berta comes and puts a hand over her mouth. Somehow she manages to get the now completely apathetic girl back into the house.

Lina is burning up with fever that evening and is taken to the hospital. She stays there for the next few days. In her feverish delirium, she dreams of a beautiful flowery meadow where she plays with her brothers and sisters. Her parents are there too and talk to her kindly: "You must be very brave in the time that is coming, it will certainly be hard for you."

In the meantime, things are very confused at the Stetten institution, and no one knows what will happen next. Rumors of closure and liquidation are going around. Ethnic Germans from the east are due to be transferred to Stetten, so the institution has to be vacated. But everything is very uncertain. No no one feels safe here anymore.

On November 12, another 43 residents are taken away, and now the place is half empty. The staff are almost out of work, and people keep asking how they can go on like this.

Finally, the evacuation is a done deal and everything has to happen very quickly. Lina feels a little better, but she still stays in the infirmary. She watches from the window as the people are taken away. A few are now being picked up by their relatives.

126

A car pulls into the yard, and a gentleman in a suit gets out. "He looks important, probably another one of the ones responsible for the takeover," says the nurse.

Everything around Lina dissolves – it is as if the whole institution slowly disappears in the fog. Reality seems to blur, and Lina takes refuge in her dreams where she is safe and not afraid. The world outside the window confuses her too much – the dull November mists don't make things any better.

On Sunday, the mood in the chapel is exceptionally subdued, because the pastor is holding a farewell service. "We all have to leave," Lina whispers to the girl next to her, "we will all be picked up …"

On November 25, another transport of people is to take place, but this time it is different from usual. Some of the caregivers and sisters also get on the buses. What would they have to do here in an empty institution? They may be needed elsewhere. They are not entirely comfortable with it, but it is war after all, and sacrifices have to be made.

Auntie Berta packs a bag with Lina's things and puts her coat on. "You're coming with me," she says, "don't be afraid, we're just moving to Winnenden – until the war is over."

"Not to the hospital!" Lina cries in horror.

"Of course not, I'm telling you, we'll still be in a castle there, in Winnenden, it's not far away, you know that. Now come, Lina."

Lina walks across the courtyard clutching Berta's hand tightly. Don't get in!" a voice buzzes in her head.

"Now come on. Look, I'm getting on the bus after all, and I'm really coming with you." The auntie does actually get on the bus. The driver has already lifted Lina up and she is sitting next to Auntie Berta with wide, frightened eyes.

"Why can't we stay here?" Lina wails.

As the bus drives off, she tries to look out the window, but the panes have been obscured with gray paint. Through a tiny hole where it has been scratched away, Lina catches a last glimpse of the Schlossberg. Slowly, the Stetten home disappears completely in the fog.

Winnenden

The trip is soon over, because Winnenden is only 15 kilometers from Stetten. Winnenden Castle shines brightly in the setting sun as the bus stops at the gate in front of the Lenau House. Lina doesn't let go of Berta's hand even when she gets off the bus, she is all confused and takes only a limited interest in her new surroundings.

There is quite a crush; here, too, no one seems to know quite what is next to be done. Finally, mattresses are handed out and taken to the gymnasium, where the new arrivals are to be given makeshift accommodation. Berta has a hard job delivering Lina there. Fortunately, she discovers Else, who still knows Lina from school.

Anxiously, the girls push their mattresses together and settle down on them. Each of them has a blanket around her shoulder, because it's anything but warm in the gym, with only a small stove at the very front.

"I want to go home," Lina complains, and Else nods agreement. Eventually a watery soup is doled out, and everyone gets a tiny piece of bread to go with it. After that Lina and Else fall into an exhausted sleep, despite the hunger and the cold.

Next day, the soup is even thinner and there is no bread at all. Lina complains to Berta in horror: "When are we going home again? Back there we sometimes even had white bread and there was a real bed."

"You have to be a little bit patient, Lina. Everything

will soon be better organized here too, just at the moment everyone is a bit overwhelmed," Berta tries to explain.

"But why does all this have to happen?" asks Lina with tears in her eyes.

"It's the war," Beate tells her.

"Always this war, I never wanted it, since then nothing has gone right. First all my friends disappear, and now I've almost disappeared, too," Lina complains.

Berta puts a second blanket around her shoulders and tries to calm her down. But Lina lies awake for a long time, still trying to understand what is happening around her.

A few days later, the girls and women are relocated to the large banquet hall in the castle. Here, too, the mattresses are laid close together, there is hardly enough room to walk. It is only marginally warmer than in the gymnasium. Lina clings to Berta's skirt and whines constantly that she wants to go home. Sometimes she takes refuge in her dreams again. For days at a time, she lies curled up on her mattress and is completely out of it.

When the doctor in charge, Dr. Gutekunst, comes to visit the women and girls in the banquet hall, he asks Lina what is the matter and why she won't get up. Lina just looks at him wearily and says: "My father said to me tonight that I should go on ahead and that I can wait for him and the others with my little brother. Where I'm going, it won't be cold anymore and I won't be hungry either."

Surprised, the doctor asks Auntie Berta what this is all about. She explains to him that Lina likes to dream about her family and gets lost in her dreams and fantasies. Thoughtfully, the doctor says: "That's not the worst solution in these terrible times."

Deportations have already taken place at the Winnenden sanatorium and nursing home. Basic trust is shaken among the remaining residents and staff. Everyone flinches when the sound of a motor is heard.

The Advent season is very different from what Lina is used to in Stetten. Efforts are made in Winnenden to create a pre-Christmas atmosphere, but the means are all too limited. At least on Advent Sundays there is an extra ration of potatoes.

Even worse than the hunger is the freezing cold. Winter is just as relentless as last year. Berta tries in vain to get Lina to go outside. "You love the snow, don't you? Look how beautiful the castle courtyard looks now."

Lina just shakes her head sorrowfully. "It's much nicer in Stetten." She has no eyes for the icy glittering world outside the window. Tired, she approaches the stove, but the best seats there have already been taken.

Christmas Day is not particularly festive. There is a little extra food and a few Christmas carols are sung. All the same, the church is packed.

In the meantime, refugees have arrived from the east. Lina looks into the worn and deathly tired faces of these people. An older woman tells her, crying, that she lost her entire family while fleeing. Lina tenderly strokes her hands and says, "Yes, I know, I have no one left either. But soon, when I have gone on ahead, they will all come back, and we will be together and happy." The woman looks hard at Lina, and feels strangely comforted by these words.

The new year has begun, and the uncomfortable atmosphere at the castle in Winnenden has not changed. Lina still asks at every opportunity when the war will finally be over and she can go home again. At least she is starting to take in her surroundings a bit more, albeit hesitantly, and is making new friends. The overworked caregivers and sisters are happy for any assistance. As far as she is able, Lina helps them a little here and there with their daily tasks. She very much enjoys taking care of the refugees, especially the children. Often she sits by a crib and rattles off her rather confused stories, or a mishmash of fairy tales. The sisters have to suppress their amusement, but they let Lina do it. In fact she succeeds in calming the children's troubled souls with her stories.

Only very slowly and imperceptibly does the cruel winter of war loosen its icy grip. It seems as if the cold has gotten into everyone's bones and souls. One morning, Lina wakes up to the sound of water drops dripping from the icicles on the roof. She quickly runs off to look for Berta. "Now it will soon be spring, then we can go home to Stetten again!" she calls to her from a distance. "And then my sisters and my father can finally come to visit me," she adds hopefully. Berta is surprised that Lina is still thinking about her family in all the confusion.

There has been no word from Lina's parents for a long time. Her father is in the war, and the siblings are all busy with their daily chores. Liesl is now 21 years old and still struggling with her bad burns. Of course she still has to see how she can make ends meet – what she needs to live, she has to earn herself. But at least there she is lucky for once, and finds a good job in the office of a big company in Heilbronn. Gertrud and Frieda are still in Lichtenstern; Fritz is back in Schwäbisch Hall and works for a farmer there. The little brothers Emil and August are both settled into their new families, and have not kept in touch with their siblings or parents. Only Elsa and Johanna, now seven and twelve years old, get regular visits from Liesl at their foster families in S. and H. Does Liesl still think about Lina from time to time?

At last, it is warm enough to get out into the fresh air again. On a mild February day, Lina walks with the others through the extensive castle grounds. The winter air does them all good.

Distracted by the new impressions, Lina has not even noticed that she has not seen Auntie Berta all day. This is very unusual, because normally Auntie is always near her. Else doesn't know either where she could be. None of the residents seems to have seen Berta.

Lina walks around uneasily for a while, and then decides to ask one of the nurses about Berta. "Oh, she left today," the sister says indifferently, "she's needed more urgently elsewhere. She probably has to report to a field hospital."

"That's not true!" cries Lina, beside herself. "She promised to stay with me, you're lying!" Her eyes open wide in horror. Screaming and crying, she runs through the corridors of the castle. "Auntie Berta, Auntie Berta!" Her shouts echo through the building. She can't and won't believe that her auntie, who has been her mother and family substitute for so many years, has actually abandoned her.

Eventually the nurses catch up with her. With Else's help, they manage to calm the girl down a bit.

Finally, Lina lies exhausted on her mattress, crying softly and unhappily to herself. But what's this? There is a package under her pillow. Astonished, Lina tears open the paper and finds the red woolen scarf that Auntie Berta herself often wore around her shoulders. There is also a note. What could the auntie have written her? Lina runs outside into the hallway. She is lucky: there is Sister Elfriede, who has a bit of a soft spot for her. Lina holds the paper out to her: "Please read it to me," she says tearfully.

My dear Lina, I can't say goodbye to you because I know how hard it would be for you — but it's not easy for me either. Please be a brave girl and don't cry. When this war is over soon, we will surely be together again. The shawl is to keep you warm until then and to remind you of me. Your Auntie Berta

"You see, it also says that you're not to cry anymore," says Sister Elfriede. "Everything will be all right. Now go back to your bed."

The days get warmer and longer. But Lina is not as cheerful as she used to be. She is now almost 17 years old, and tries desperately to make sense of what has been happening around her in the last few weeks. It's all so confusing. She longs for the security of the past, when she still lived carefree at the castle in Stetten. Everything there was so familiar to her. Now she clings all the more to Else, the only person here she has known for any length of time. The two girls have become good friends and are always out and about together.

No sooner are the ice and snow thawed, and the roads passable again, than the old fear of the gray buses returns. Once again, people shiver and hide every time an engine is heard.

"How can you be expected to live in peace if you always have to be afraid," Else complains one day. "if they would just finally take us all away and kill us, then we wouldn't have to be frightened anymore!"

"But why should they want to kill us when we haven't done anything?" Lina asks, shocked. She has never seen her friend this way before – she finds it quite disturbing.

"Actually we should just run away. We're not little kids anymore, after all," says Else thoughtfully.

"Why don't we just go back to Stetten? It's not that far, we only drove a short distance in the bus," whispers Lina.

The idea is born, and from now on the friends are constantly putting their heads together. They think from every angle about how and when they can put their plan into action.

One evening in March they finally see their opportunity.

"Lina and Else, you take the dishes back to the kitchen," orders one of the sisters.

"Yes, right away!" Else calls out to her and gives Lina a sign. Quickly, each of the girls stuffs a small bundle under their coats, then they set off with the tub of dishes. Lina actually wants to go down the stairs to the kitchen, but Else snaps at her, "Are you stupid? Leave the stuff here and get out fast!" They put the tub down in the hallway and run out through an open side door into the castle grounds, now almost dark.

The two runaways quickly realize that it is still quite cold at night. Arriving at the end of the castle park, they are already freezing. Lina has wrapped the red shawl around her head, but her feet in her thin boots are ice cold. Else is no better. "Maybe we should have waited till the spring after all?" she complains. But it's too late to do anything about it now.

Finally the girls discover an old woodshed and are glad to find that the door is not locked. But inside it is just as cold as outside. Miserably, they squat on the ground and huddle together. They have found a few old sacks to cover themselves with.

Lina has weird dreams. Auntie Berta is standing next to a gray bus, waving, and kindly urges her to get on. "No, don't get on!" cries Lina and wakes up. No sooner has she fallen back asleep than she dreams she hears the buses approaching. She wakes up again.

Else is also awake. "It's just too cold," she says, shaking her head, "and we don't even know the way to Stetten. I'm hungry, too – come on, let's go back, it's already light outside."

Lina agrees. Slowly, they walk back toward the castle. They rack their brains about what they could say in their defense. "We'll just say we got lost," Else decides.

The castle grounds are already quite busy. Despite the early hour, many people are out and about. Now Lina sees the reason – there are two gray buses at the gate and the nurses are already taking some residents in that direction.

"Quick, we'll have to run for it!" cries Else. She turns around and runs right into the arms of Sister Elfriede.

"Ah, there you are at last," she says. She grabs the girls roughly by the arm and drags them to the Lenau House.

Here they are handed their bundles and an orderly writes a number on each person's upper arm. 45318, this number is also on the list that the nurse checks off. Most of them are followed by a big "+", Lina's among them. However, Else must have somehow gotten in the way, because the list says "Else Bernhardt" and not "Karoline Bernhardt". Lina is completely stunned and can't utter a word, not even her name. She no longer notices how frantically most of the deportees refuse to get on the bus.

For a brief second, hope springs up in her: *Maybe they're taking us back to Stetten?* she thinks.

But there are so many people from Winnental here – what would they be doing in Stetten?

Lina and Else sit exhausted next to each other on the bus. What with the icy night in the woodshed and now this abrupt departure, the girls are completely worn out.

The trip takes quite a while, so they're not going back to Stetten. Since the windows are again obscured with paint, they can't look out. The engine noise makes them tired, and eventually they both fall asleep.

Lina dreams of a warm room with a nice big stove in

it, friendly people sitting on soft, comfortable sofas and smiling at her. A woman says, "Soon everything will be fine, Lina, and then you'll be able to join us."

Weinsberg, 10 March 1941

When the bus finally stops and the doors are opened, it is still broad daylight. The sun is shining on a spacious park. There is no castle here, but Lina sees several beautifully structured brick buildings among the trees and lawns. They are led into one of these.

They enter a large hall in which many women and girls are already accommodated on mattresses. Else quickly pulls Lina to her and sighs, "If only we could be lying in our beds in Stetten again."

Finally there is something to eat. The girls are totally famished, they gobble down the soup and bread without hesitation. Afterwards they feel a little better. Else has thoughts of escape again, but Lina doesn't listen to her. She stands by the window and watches as the sun slowly sets behind the park. The sun's rays illuminate the lawns, on which the first tender green has begun to show.

Conditions in Weinsberg are even worse than in Winnenden; here, too, there is an atmosphere of fear and terror. It is an endless coming and going – patients come, and others are taken away. The gray buses are very well known here and the fear is a constant presence; the agitation of the patients is almost unbearable. The few sisters and orderlies are overworked, they seem quite lost and unhappy. Even the senior physician, Dr. Joos, who makes the rounds in the evening, seems depressed, as if the burden he has to carry has become much too great. Nobody really wanted it to be like this in Weinsberg.

Desperate attempts are made to maintain a minimum of order and something like a daily schedule. But the food is absolutely inadequate. All sectors are experiencing cutbacks – most of all the "loony bins". The soldiers need bread and beds – such valuable resources can't be wasted on the "useless" sick. The most hopeless cases are reduced to "death rations" – they get only broth made from vegetables, without fat or bread. In the long run this is enough to kill them by starvation.

Lina has totally withdrawn into herself. If she talks at all, it's only about her dreams and fantasies. "Auntie Berta picked me up today, we walked through a flowery meadow and I picked a big bunch of flowers. Then we took it to my mother, because she's in hospital," she says one morning.

Else just shakes her head sadly, she can't cope with Lina anymore. She just tells stories like that, and talks about people who aren't even there. But the fact that she has lost interest in eating is not a bad thing for Else. She quickly gobbles up Lina's portions along with her own.

March is drawing to a close. One morning the sun shines with unusual warmth, and the nurses encourage some of the sick to go for a walk. A nice young nurse tries to persuade Lina to get up.

"No, I can't," says Lina, "I have to wait for my little brother. He was here last night and said I would finally be able to go with him, and then everything will be fine again."

The sister puts her hand on Lina's forehead and says gently, "You seem a little feverish, you'd better rest."

Sadly, on her way out, she looks back at the young girl lying curled up on the mattress – just yesterday she saw the transport list. Lina's name was on it.

The decision of the District Welfare Office of June 1940 states that payment will be made for Lina up until March 31, 1941. Can this really be a coincidence?

31 March 1941

Early in the morning, the buses are waiting in front of the main building in Weinsberg. It is a beautiful sunny spring day. Already the usual terror starts – people have to be brought to the buses. The numbers on their arms have been redone, the bundles of clothes have long since been distributed. Everyone is supposed to have a quick drink. "Where are you taking us? What is going to become of us?" some cry out. "You'll see, you'll like it there," the men who came with the buses answer, indifferently.

Lina doesn't notice any of this, she can hardly walk anymore and the young nurse leads her to the bus with tears in her eyes. As she gets on board, an emotion flickers up in Lina once again: *Don't get on!* She thinks she sees Horstle and Helene standing next to the bus, both shaking their heads frantically. But she no longer has the strength to resist. Already Else, who tries to struggle, has been pushed into the bus and the doors close. Again it all happens very quickly.

The journey goes on and on. It is long past noon, people are hungry and thirsty. The wailing and crying gets louder. The orderlies give those who are making too much noise an injection.

Lina doesn't make a sound; she sits upright in her seat and gazes with interest at the darkened windows. A smile is on her face as she watches a beautiful landscape pass by outside. Sunny meadows with colorful flowers, fields, trees full of fruit and green forests. Also a sparkling lake and – oh, there are people too, happily laughing people, people waving! Everyone is cheerful and looks happy. What a beautiful world. "Wait," Lina calls out to them in her dream, "I want to stay with you, wait for me!" The people look strangely familiar to her, although she can't remember seeing them before. "You can't come with us yet, first you have to go through the gate!" they call. "What gate?" Lina wants to ask, but then she wakes abruptly.

The bus has arrived.

Hadamar

The doors open, but it is not at all light outside. The bus is parked in a wooden shack. Strange nurses help her get off. Lina has to be supported again, she can hardly hold herself up. Through a side door they enter a building, where they are told to undress so they can be examined by the doctor. After that they will take a shower, and when they been good and completed these procedures, they will have a nice dinner.

A nurse helps Lina undress. Because the girl is shaking so much, she puts a coat around her shoulders. Then Lina is standing in a room. Strange people are seated there and a man in a white coat takes hold of her – bends her head to the side, looks into her mouth. Only very briefly and in surprise does she come back momentarily to awareness of her surroundings.

"Is this a hospital?" It is too much for her brain to take in. "Where is the gate?" she murmurs.

"Just come with me." Another nurse shepherds her out of the room.

Together with many other women and girls, she is pushed down a staircase and finally enters a black and white tiled room with a shower head on the wall. Lina and Else are pushed into a corner. The room is far too crowded.

The heavy door closes shut with a bang. No water comes out of the shower head. The women begin to gasp for air, some scream in panic and hammer on the door in mortal terror.

It becomes more and more difficult to breathe and they pull and tug at each other. Lina leans against the wall, finally seeing the heavenly landscape appear in front of her again. This time it is even brighter and more beautiful. And there it is – Lina has never seen anything so beautiful – a gate of gold, it sparkles and shines in an incredible light. In the middle of the gate her little brother is standing.

"Come on, Lina, now you're home at last," he calls. Lina walks toward the gate – she slides down the cold wall and falls onto the other lifeless women and girls. Next to her, Else tries to pull herself up once more. Lina's head falls to the side and there is a smile on her face.

Her little brother has spread his arms wide and Lina runs as fast as she can through the gate towards him.

The End

The Hadamar death factory

In 1883 a penal institution began operating in Hadamar. In 1906 it was repurposed to become the state sanatorium. At the beginning of the Second World War, the Wehrmacht used the building as a reserve hospital. At the end of 1940, the "T4" head office had alterations made to the state sanatorium in order to use it as a killing center for the "Action T4" extermination campaign. A gas chamber, a dissection room and two incinerators were installed, and a bus garage was built.

Gray buses picked up the patients from the "intermediate institutions" (Andernach, Eichberg, Galkhausen, Herborn, Idstein, Scheuern, Weilmünster, Weinsberg and Wiesloch), where they had been temporarily housed for a few weeks.

After arrival in Hadamar, the patients were made to get out in the closed bus garage and were led into the main building. There they had to undress and present themselves to the doctor. On the basis of the accompanying patient file, the doctor determined an allegedly natural cause of death for the death certificate to be issued later. The patients were then led by nurses and orderlies to the gas chamber in the basement.

Their corpses were disposed of by the "furnaces" in the two crematorium ovens. The relatives received a "comfort letter" informing them of the patient's sudden demise. The death, supposedly due to illness, was presented as a blessed release. The urn which would be sent on request did not contain – contrary to what was stated – the ashes of the murdered person.

From 13 January to 24 August 1941, over 10,000 victims died in the Hadamar gas chamber.

During the "Second Murder Phase", the former Hadamar state sanatorium once again assumed the function of a killing facility. From August 1942 to 26 March 1945, nearly 4,500 more victims died there. Those who did not succumb quickly enough to the deliberate starvation diet or the withheld medical care were killed by overdosed medication. The doctor, head nurse and head orderly decided each morning which patients should die. The night shift then administered the lethal drugs to the selected victims. Their bodies were buried in mass graves in the specially constructed sanatorium cemetery. The patients were brought to Hadamar in large transports from all over the Reich. Among them were forced laborers from the former Soviet Union and Poland as well as children with one Jewish parent.

Of the staff in Hadamar, five doctors, an administrative director, and both female and male nursing staff were actively involved in the murders between 1941 and 1945. They had to answer for the crimes they had committed in two post-war trials. After the war, the victims were not recognized as the objects of persecution by the Nazi regime and so did not receive any reparations.

(http://www.gedenkstaette-hadamar.de, accessed 07.28.2012)

Afterword

From left to right: Ruth Alice Dunkelmann,
Elsa Dunkelmann née Bernhardt, Brigitte Wege

What really happened back then? Where was Lina taken? Could I still find out something about her after 70 years?

These are the questions I asked myself at the beginning of my search for my unknown aunt. My mother and her many siblings grew up under difficult circumstances. Some of them only got to know each other as adults.

Only Lina seemed to have vanished completely.

For my mother, my sister and me, in searching for her it was as if we were at last gradually getting to know her, and above all coming to love her.

Ruth Alice Dunkelmann